# School Daze

Six Tales of Science Fantasy

Robert E. Hampson

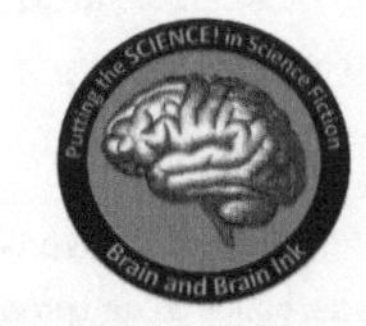


Brain and Brain Ink

# Contents

For Ruann, the love of my life; for Mom, my first fan; and for Dad, my hero and role model.

A special thanks and dedication to "Uncle Timmy" Bolgeo who always thought I should write under my real name.

# Additional Copyright Information

# Foreword

I am often asked how I came to use the pen-name Tedd Roberts, and then, how I came to drop the pen-name and use my own. I was in mid-career as a scientist; I was an associate professor hoping to make tenure and professorship, and a bit worried about how it would look have published science fiction stories (when my colleagues might think that I *should* have been writing *science*). In addition, there was an incident where the agency funding our work scoured social media for unauthorized communications about the research program. I was actually quite happy I'd used a nickname given to me by an old friend, and my real first name, to create Tedd Roberts. In fact, I'd been using it for more than ten years by that point to keep my online activity private and separate from my professional work. The first four stories I sold professionally were written as Tedd, as were my blog, and about half of the science articles I wrote for Baen.

Nowadays, when asked why I dropped the pen-name, I usually answer "I got tenure." While it is true that being a full Professor allows me a certain comfort in revealing my writing, it's also the case that I've been able to show that my presence in SF circles allows me to bring a unique perspective to teaching, particularly when it comes to communicating science to the public. It's outreach, I promise!

In reality, though, the name change dates to LibertyCon 28, in 2015—well, technically, it dates to 2014, when it was announced at LC27 that I would be

Science Guest of Honor at next year's LibertyCon in Chattanooga, TN. The SF convention was founded by Tim "Uncle Timmy" Bolgeo, an engineer for the Tennessee Valley Authority, and SF fan. Uncle Timmy was friends with many scientists and engineers, and LibertyCon has had a strong science track for decades. The day before the 2015 GoHs were to be announced, Uncle Timmy asked permission to announce me by my real name, reasoning that since my science credentials were as Robert E. Hampson, then I should be Science GoH under that name.

Promotion and tenure came later, but the beginning of the end for Tedd Roberts was that warm Tennessee Saturday in June of 2014. Here then, are the collected scribblings of Tedd, under his *real* name!

# LOWER EDUCATION

*Authors note: These stories take place in various educational settings, from grade-school to graduate school, and reflect some of the author's thoughts on education in a science fiction/fantasy world. For example, what if the failings of a school system didn't lie with the administrators, but with...other entities? We might be looking at a case of lower education.*

No matter how hard I tried, it just wasn't possible to block out the sounds of a 13-year-old boy arriving home from school.

"Mom, I think my teacher is an Alien."

I was working in my home office, but Steve's voice carried throughout the whole house. It certainly got my attention. I turned down the music in time to hear my wife's quieter voice correct him: "Of course Patrick, there are lots of immigrants teaching in our schools."

"No Mom, an *illegal* alien."

"Patrick, that's not nice.  I'm sure there are no undocumented workers at your school."

"Mo-om, I mean a SPACE alien, like Mister Spock, but not so nice."

I had decided it was time for a break.  I'd come home from the lab to write my research grant application and had gotten a lot of work done.  I had the rest of the weekend to do the proof-reading, so I could afford some rest.  As I entered the kitchen, I asked: "What makes you say that, Ricky?"

"Well, Mister O'Connor handed out the test papers and told us he didn't want to see us looking around at other kid's papers.  Then he went to his cabinet and was looking in some sort of mirror and he just kinda 'fuzzed.'"

"Fuzzed?"

"Yeah, like on TV, whenever they want to imitate a hologram, it looks kind of 3-D, but then it fuzzes, and wiggles around, then snaps back into focus."

"And just what were *you* doing looking around?  Especially since he told you not to."

"He's just gotten creepy, Dad.  I couldn't help it."

"So did he see you?"

"Uh, yeah, I guess so."  Ricky reached into his pocket and pulled out a piece of blue paper that had been folded down to about an inch on a side.  "I'm s'posed to give this to you."

I unfolded the paper into a standard letter-sized page and read the notice that "Patrick Harris received a failing grade on his Algebra test because of cheating" and would I please meet with the teacher and vice-principal on Monday.

Monday wasn't a great day. The grant application had to be submitted around noon, and there was a lot to be done. Finally, the Sponsored Research Office and I had the application completed and submitted. It looked like I would make it to the 2 o'clock meeting after all.

Instead of being ushered into the Vice-Principal's office, I was led to a small conference room filled with not just the VP and Algebra teacher, but all of Patrick's core curriculum teachers, and the district assistant superintendent. "Professor Harris," began the VP, "we have a problem with Patrick."

"Patrick is insolent," said the English teacher.

"He's a smart-ass," corrected the Science teacher, "he argues with all of the students and rejects the accepted State Science Curriculum."

"He has no appreciation of the *process* for completing his Social Studies pro-jects."

"Mister Harris," hissed the assistant superintendent in a low voice.

"That's *Doctor* Harris, Sir."

"Yesssss, Doctor Harrisssss. You sssssee, this program is for highly academically gifted sssssstudentsssss. Your sssssson is impeding their progresssss. He must leave the program. I will leave you" he pointed to the VP "to sssssettle thisssss."

The teachers left me alone with the VP. "Mister Judge, Patrick's a good kid, he's gotten good grades until now.

"Doctor Harris, I sympathize. I have enjoyed having both of your sons in this school, but I can't ignore the teacher evaluations. I have reports here—Patrick refuses to show his work in Math, claims he can calculate the answer in his head. He argued with the Science teacher and students over scientific evidence regarding pesticide and fluorocarbon bans. He called the Social Studies teacher a Socialist, and refused to complete an English project making African Tribal Masks."

"Wait a minute—were his answers wrong?  Did he show proper literature citations?  The Social Studies teacher *is* a Socialist, she gave him a failing grade on his Constitution paper about the Second Amendment, and what do African Tribal Masks have to do with English grammar and American Literature?"

"That's irrelevant Doctor Harris.  Modern education is about the process not the outcome.  I'm afraid they are right.  Patrick must move to a different school.  I suggest the military academy in Oak Ridge."

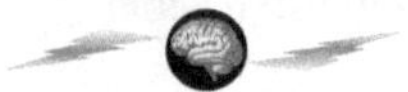

The day got worse when Brian arrived home unexpectedly from college.

"Dad, I'm dropping out.  The Neanderthals in the Biology department have decided we can't even do dissections any more.  I can't take it; I'd rather write Science Fiction."

But it was all overshadowed by the news that night.  It had happened.  There was intelligent life out there in the Universe.  Communications had been established.  The first envoy would be here in a couple months and they wanted to visit Earth's scientific and educational institutions to see if we were eligible for membership in their galactic society.

*That* would show the educators who was right.  We'd survive.  I got Patrick transferred to a private school and Brian was enrolled in an on-line degree program.  Let him get an associates and work for a few years.

We were fortunate to be selected for one of the scientific tours for our new friends, The *Hyssssst*.  Our neural computing facility, the prosthetics group, and the tissue engineering institute had caught their attention, so we had to prepare a dog and pony show for the Ambassador and a group of scientific advisors.

It took about six months to set up the visit. Toward the end, I corresponded pretty regularly with my counterpart Tar-Yrl, who had the equivalent of a *Hyssssst* doctorate in neural medicine. Near as I could figure out, he was a professor at a major research institute and had been attached to the Embassy to help evaluate Earth's scientific progress. Once the tour had finished in our area I found that I had a few minutes alone with Tar. I felt I knew him well enough to talk about subjects other than our immediate scientific interests, so I told him my concerns about educating our children to be productive citizens of galactic society.

I was shocked by his reaction. I realize I shouldn't have made assumptions about an alien race, but I was pretty sure that grimace was a smile and the head nod meant agreement. Tar seemed to be approving of the teachers!

I couldn't believe it, so I asked: "Tar how can you approve of a system that teaches kids to be mediocre and ignore real education?" But as I listened to his answer it hit me where I'd heard that type of voice before.

"Friend Harrisssss. You misssssundersssssstand. We don't *want* you to be educated."

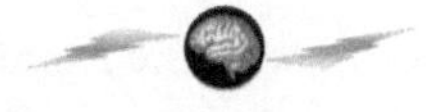

# You Built WHAT?

*Authors note: Artificial Intelligence is a hot topic. Some welcome our inevitable computer overlords. (Thank you, Skynet!). Others fear it.*

*But how will we know when a computer program is truly intelligent?*

*On the flip side—are we? Really?*

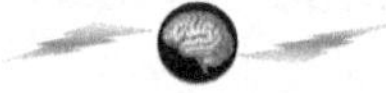

"It's not the *job* I hate," wrote Steward. "Sure, committee meetings were a literal pain in the butt, budget reviews were disheartening, and student seminars were an exercise in patience. No, it was the... OK, yes, it's the *job* I hate.

"'The duties and responsibilities of Department Chair include the bidirectional representation of faculty concerns with the Administration, and the enforcement of Institutional Policies and Procedures with the faculty and staff of the Department'—Institutional Policy and Procedures Manual, 214th Edition.

"Yeah, that's the one. Riding herd on the faculty. Have you ever known a worse collection of screw-ups, screw-offs and prima donnas, Russ? I suppose you have, you worked here once too. Things were *so* much easier when we were grad students. I suppose I should explain. But first, are there any openings up there, Russ? I know the Federal Budget is tight. Heaven knows I know that, just from looking at the NIH budgets, but I've got to get out of here!"

It started because of the request for the supercomputing center...

"Hey Boss, didja see this?" Professor Leon Barrons didn't even bother knocking on the door to his department chairman's office, just barged in, as he'd done ever since they'd shared an office as Assistant Professors. "Comp center wants models to test the new hypernodal cluster. I should give them the ENURON model."

"Leon, *why* haven't you changed that name? It was just a typo by a summer student."

"Hey, he was a writer; it was funny. Besides, he came up with a decent acronym: Electronic Neural Unit Recursive Omnigenic Node. I *told* you that, Steward."

"You made that up after the fact. 'Omnigenic' isn't even a real word in Neuroscience." Prof Barrons' teaching reviews were filled with juicy tidbits such as "Entertaining lecturer," "engaging speaker," and the inevitable "Does he just make this stuff up?" Leon was the most popular teacher in the introductory class for non-majors, and the least popular teacher in the graduate program. His haphazard style just did not impress students who had to pay meticulous attention to detail for the five to seven years until their dissertations were complete.

"Sure, it is, 'omni' for 'universal' and 'genic' for 'source'. The 'omnigenic' model uses the universal source code of each brain cell to write information." Leon stated with a smug look on his face. Steward just sighed. He'd caught himself doing that a lot lately.

"Very well. You can use one Research Assistant for ten hours a week. That's all the departmental budget will allow, we only have three second year students on assistantships this semester, and the Stroke Center Training Grant states that they need to spend at least twenty hours per week on the Stroke and Brain Injury Project."

The problem with neural models was complexity. Each square micrometer of membrane of a brain cell controlled the diffusion of at least 5 different ions—those small chemical molecules that had positive or negative charge. Five ions, and channels that allowed them in or out, was ten channels. Then there were calculations for inside and outside the cell—that made twenty calculations. Multiply that by approximately 100,000 square microns of membrane per neuron meant over two million calculations per neuron, and that didn't even include the inputs and outputs! A complete neural model of more than one neuron at a time required more computation than a single computer could deliver. The new computing center advertised 1000 main processors, with a new annex consisting of arrays of 1000 general purpose processing units per main processor. Barrons estimated that with a million processing components, he and his students could easily model up to 10 million neurons at a time.

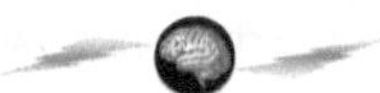

"What's this?" Barrons had been waiting for Steward when he returned to his office, and handed him a single sheet of paper.

"It's the result from the latest run from the ENURON model" replied Barrons, pointing to the two words on the paper.

"'Cheese, please?' Don't waste my time, Leon, I just came from the Dean's Office and he said we have to cut non-research salary support of any professor not pulling their own weight in teaching."

"No, really. We modeled ten million neurons. That's the size of a mouse brain. Once the calculations started, it printed this, and the core calculations started jumping around the nodes just like a rat running a maze. "

"Unbelievable."

"'Woof?'" Steward sighed. "You hired that Hoyt kid back and he's working on this project isn't he, Leon?"

"Honest, Steward. This is what we got when we modeled 100 million neurons. It was a bit slow on the computer until they added another node of 1000 GPPUs. It's really strange to see those network cables wagging."

"'Ook?' What's this smudge?"

"Waste ink. It collects on the bottom of the printer. I think it's the computer equivalent to throwing excrement."

Sigh. "How many neurons, Leon?"

"Anywhere from a quarter to half a billion. The size of a small primate. The tie-in with the cluster at State is incredible."

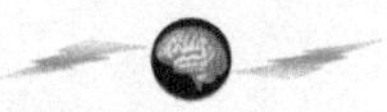

"This is serious. I need to know what has the Dean so upset and why the computer center says we aren't allowed to connect to the National Universities' network? Do you realize they want to take the damages out of *our* budget, Leon?"

"Two billion neurons, Steward. It was incredible. With the entire net at our disposal, plus the idle time on every student laptop, we modeled enough neurons to build a human brain."

"And?"

Leon didn't speak, but simply handed over the printed page.

Contract requirements:

200 sq ft office

1000 sq ft lab

Tenure

"Oh God, Leon. How could you? Another *faculty* member?"

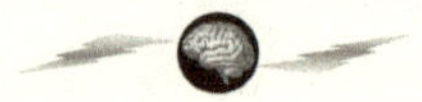

# BLOOD SCIENCE

*Authors note:  An author friend challenged me to write a story in all variations of the SF/F genre in retaliation for me telling her "I don't write that kind of story." The subgenre in question was Urban Fantasy.  I put my own twist on it by making it City-University Fantasy, and taking a potshot at the author herself! Some might also notice a certain trope being abused in this story as well.*

*Hmm, when you think about it, I guess blood really could be the perfect food source.* Teddy sat at a computer in his home office staring at a blank word processing screen. *Elise thinks I'm too much of a scientist to write a vampire story, but I'm going to do it just because of the challenge.  I have to come up with a reason though.*

For the past 10 years he had taken time away from family and work to write a few words of science fiction here and there, trying to sell some short stories and work up to that Big Debut Novel. In the previous two years he had corresponded with several SF authors and attended a few conventions in which the emphasis had been on writing, rather than movies, TV and video games.  More recently he'd begun corresponding with Elise, a moderately successful fantasy and science fiction author.  Elise believed Teddy had talent, but his characters tended to fall too much into the stereotypes of either scientists or Boy Scouts.  Teddy argued that he had to write what he knew.  Twenty-five years as a professor and scientist had left its mark, hence his current obsession with trying to write a vampire story based on logic and science.

*Blood carries oxygen, glucose, small proteins and essential nutrients to all of the cells in the body. If I postulate a disease that affects a person's ability to metabolize complex foods, then it could be logical that the creature would turn to human blood to fulfill its nutritional needs.* Teddy tapped a few keys, started an internet browser on his computer and pulled up a national database of medical literature. *Cystic Fibrosis affects the digestion, but our fictional vampire wouldn't last long with the side effects on the lungs. Some form of gastrointestinal parasite? Or maybe a virus that blocks absorption. That way it could be contagious about 1% of the time, accounting for a vampire bite turning the victim into a vampire.*

Teddy typed a few notes into his word processor, wrote an introductory paragraph and outlined the next couple paragraphs, but didn't yet know which direction he wanted to take the story. He had a department faculty meeting tomorrow evening and would be late coming home. He'd think about it for a couple of days and perhaps get back to the story next weekend.

It was more than 3 weeks before he got back to working on his story. Despite best intentions to get up a little earlier each morning, exercise and spend at least 30 minutes writing, he found himself occupied with work and emails with colleagues later each night. After one extreme evening of grant and manuscript writing, he found himself going to bed as his wife was getting up for an early start at work. As a result, all intentions of early morning activity were lost to catching up on sleep.

It was late afternoon, working on evening. The latest grant application had been submitted and yet another scientific manuscript had been sent off to the editor. With about 45 minutes to call his own, Teddy returned to the topic of the vampire story.

*Oh-kay. Blood as a food source to replace essential nourishment. Our fictional vampire is going to want the blood as clean as possible. Iron rich, low cholesterol... hmm, add in a bit of estrogen for the antiaging effects and their natural food source would be young women. Huh. To keep the potential contaminants down, make that "nubile" young women. That's another stereotype down. Now, how to kill a vampire...*

Intent on the story outline, Teddy didn't notice the pale graduate student standing in the door. Wondering if his advisor would ever look up from his typing, the student decided to knock discretely.

"Wha'? Oh, John, sorry, I was involved in this outline."

"Another grant? Something that can pay for another technician in the lab? I really need some help in the daytime." John was studying sleep cycles in rats and needed to perform most of his experiments during the night when rodents were most active.

"Not yet, that particular grant should be reviewed this week. Once I know for certain how it scored, I'll post a position for the daytime tech."

"Oh, good. Thanks. Actually, I came to ask if you could talk to the committee about my Comps?" John was due to take the Comprehensive Qualifying Exam that would allow him to start working on his Ph.D. "With this all-night experiment schedule, it would be a lot easier if I could just take the Comps at night. I could come in, start the experiment, then go to the conference room for the exam. We get breaks every two hours, and that would be sufficient to check on the experiments. Nigel and Keisha are checking with their advisors, too. If would be a lot better for us, after all, you're the one that taught us about the dangers of disrupting an established sleep-wake cycle. Prof. Rose is willing to proctor the exam overnight, so we just need the committee's permission."

"I don't know, John." He frowned and continued. "I'm not entirely comfortable with you students working all night out of the eye of the professors. We had a few unfortunate incidents when I was a student..."

"I know. You've told us all about the homeless dude in the restroom and the guy that accidently killed himself. It's okay, we're not alone. There're the security guards, and Profs. Rose and Tepes. They have to run experiments late at night to avoid vibrations from the traffic outside and construction of the new hospital tower." John paused, and pushed back his long black hair. "After all, it's not like we're trying to avoid you—you told us yourself that you used to work until 5 AM, catch 4 hours sleep, then be right back for a lab meeting. It's just until we get these experiments done."

"Okay. I'll talk to the committee. They're meeting tomorrow at 5, so I will see about it then."

"Great! Thanks, Doc!" John left so fast; Teddy barely saw him go.

*That kid needs a girlfriend.* Thought his advisor. *So pale and thin. I'd worry about his health, but he's been the best player on the departmental volleyball team for the past two years. Just doesn't get out in the sun much.*

*Sun. Yeah, Vampires drink blood, so they'd have extra hemoglobin breakdown products in the body. Hyperbilirubinemia. It makes a person sensitive to sunlight. That's another one down.*

*Silver bullets? Stakes through the heart, cutting off the head? Those are all pretty obvious ways to kill anyone, let alone a vampire. Holy water and religious symbols? Make that a myth. Fast healing, though... I've got to figure out a reason why they'd be hard to kill.*

*Hmm. For now, just leave it that they heal fast. They'd have to have pretty good control of clotting and bleeding factors to keep from contaminating their food source. Yeah. Control your own bleeding and you could survive quite a bit of damage.*

Teddy stopped typing as the phone rang. "Yeah, honey, just finishing up. It is? Wow. Okay, I forgot. I'll meet you at the concert." He replaced the phone, tapped a few keys, saved the outline and turned off his computer. "I'm late, I'm late, for a very important date..." he muttered as he left the office.

Teddy pulled his car into a numbered parking spot, grabbed his lunch, a notebook, and several portable memory drives. Inside the building, he checked the mail room and stuck his head in his secretary's office.

"Afternoon, Jen." He called out.

"Good morning, you mean, Doc," she responded cheerfully. It was their usual joke. Jeannette's secretarial duties were shared by the three Assistant Professors in the department, but the other two faculty seldom showed up before mid-afternoon.

Jeannette looked a lot like the stereotype of a 50's era school teacher, but was the ideal person for organizing the schedules, mail and manuscripts of the admittedly most disorganized of the departmental faculty. "Would you like your messages, now? Or are you going to retreat to your office for 30 minutes and then call and interrupt me in the middle of my lunch break?" Fortunately, she asked it with a smile to show she wasn't really upset.

"Sure, give it to me straight, Jen."

"Okay, Journal of Neurochem wants to know when they can expect their review, you're two weeks late. Journal of Behavioral Pharmacology says you're... three weeks late with their review. The Office of Research reminds you that you have a progress report due on your sleep cycle grant in three days. Doctor Rose wants to know if you'll switch lectures with him next week, and you have a call from 'Russ in D.C.' no last name, just said you'd know who it was."

"Thanks, Jen." I handed her one of the memory drives. "The reviews are on here, 'JNC' and 'JBP' files under 'Reviews.' Put the progress report due date on my calendar, and check if I've got any conflicts with Geoff's class. I don't mind switching as long as it's clear."

"The calendar items are done, and the class period is clear. You'll be happier with his nine A.M. class than the 5 P.M. one any way. I know you're happier writing in the early evening. Don't forget 'Russ from D.C.' and you're meeting with the students at four o'clock."

"Thanks, Jen."

Once in his office, Teddy inserted the memory drive into his computer and printed out the latest version of his story. He had to get to work on that progress report, but surely he could spend a few minutes proofreading what he wrote last night.

*ROBBERTS LOOKED AROUND AT THE BLOODY SCENE.*

*"VAMPIRES? YOU THINK VAMPIRES DID THIS?" SHE LOOKED AT THE POLICEMAN IN DISBELIEF. "HAVEN'T *ANY* OF YOU PEOPLE READ MY BOOK?"*

*SHE CARRIED IT WITH HER LIKE A SHIELD ANY TIME SHE GOT CALLED OUT TO ONE OF THESE SCENES. EVEN NOW IT WAS VISIBLE STICKING OUT OF THE TOP OF HER BACKPACK: 'BLOOD SCIENCE: THE MEDICAL TRUTH ABOUT VAMPIRES BY PROF. MARY SUE ROBBERTS, M.D. PH.D.'*

*"LOOK, OFFICER, TO A VAMPIRE, BLOOD IS FOOD. IT'S LIFE. THERE ARE ESSENTIAL NUTRIENTS THAT IT CAN'T GET ANY OTHER WAY. THIS... THIS IS WASTEFUL. A HUNGRY VAMPIRE WOULD NEVER LET THIS MUCH BLOOD*

*GET AWAY. IT'S LIKE GOING FOR FAST FOOD, ORDERING A CHEESEBURGER, THEN SMEARING IT ALL OVER YOURSELF INSTEAD OF EATING IT.*

*"I MEAN, YOU WOULDN'T LEAVE DONUTS ALL OVER YOUR PATROL CAR..." SHE STOPPED AS SHE LOOKED CLOSELY AT THE TRAIL OF POWDERED SUGAR THAT STARTED ABOUT AN INCH BELOW THE OFFICER'S DOUBLE CHINS AND TRAILED DOWN OVER HIS RATHER LARGE BELLY.*

Teddy pulled out a red pen and started writing in the margin. "Needs a better intro. Too slow." He struck out the reference to the book title, then wrote:

*"VAN HELSING AIN'T GOT NOTHING ON ME." THOUGHT PROF. MARY SUE ROBBERTS, VAMPIRE HUNTER AND AUTHOR OF "BLOOD SCIENCE: THE MEDICAL TRUTH ABOUT VAMPIRES."*

He set the printout aside and got to work on the yearly report for his sleep research. Later that afternoon, once the lab meeting with students was over, he returned to editing his manuscript, but was quickly interrupted by Professor Tepes.

"Theodorrrrre. Could I haff just a moment?" Tepes' heavy accent revealed his Romanian origins, as did his particular approach to hygiene. Never a favorite of the students, they had taken to calling him "Vlad the Impaler" after an incident where he had accidently stuck himself with a hypodermic in the process of injecting one of the lab animals.

"Sure, Emil. Sit down. "

"T'anks. I just vant to ask if you could talk to the students in your class about my lab space? I don't mind them using it during the day. I only need it at night, but they need to do a better job of cleaning and restocking during the day."

"Okay. I'll talk to them. Maybe I can get Jen to make up some signs."

"T'anks, Theodorrrrre." Tepes said as he left.

Teddy reached over and turned on the small fan beside his desk. Emil had a certain... "air" about him. Probably something in his diet. A little extra air circulation wouldn't hurt, either.

*Now there is someone that would make a perfect vampire—black, greasy hair, widow's peak, thick eastern-European accent. If only he wasn't so... so unpleasant to be around. I just can't picture him having his way with a nubile maiden.*

*But what if it's all an act? A clever disguise? Yeah. I can use that! What better way for a vampire to hide, than to purposefully drive people away? Sort of like an undercover cop masquerading as a homeless person. Right. I need to find a place to work that in.*

Teddy started writing in the margins of his manuscript, oblivious to the time until the phone rang. He looked at the phone, looked at the clock, started to reach for the phone... and stopped.

"Sorry dear. I must have just left when you called." He hastily stuffed the manuscript and memory drive into his backpack, turned out the lights, and was out of the office door before the phone stopped ringing.

**Ring! Ring!**

Teddy reached for the bedside phone. It was on his side and not Trish's, since she wasn't likely to be getting calls from students in the middle of the night. He made an effort to not sound sleepy, but couldn't stifle a yawn, "Yeah, um, ah. Oh. Hello? "

"Doc, this Mike with Building Security. I hate to disturb you at three AM, but there's an alarm sounding in your lab."

"Hmm? Uh, yeah. Prob'ly the freezer. Was 'ere a power blip? "

"Yes, sir. That thunderstorm this evening knocked out the power for about 30 minutes. The emergency generators took a minute or two to kick in, but we've had power since midnight."

"S'okay. Prob'ly tripped a breaker. Jus' tell John to hit the reset. S'long as he doesn't open th'door it should be good 'til I get there in the morning. There's nothin' crit'cal in there and the rest doesn' have to stay at minus eighty. "

"Doc, that's the problem. John's not here. None of them are here. The usual night owls didn't come in this evening."

Teddy finally came awake with this latest information.

"None of them? Doctor Rose? Doctor Tepes? John or Nigel? What about that Goth girl, what's her name, Keisha?"

"No sir, this is the first night in the three years I've been working third shift that I haven't seen anyone else here. It's kind of creepy if you ask me."

"Okay. I'll be right there, in about 20 minutes. No wait..." Teddy looked at the clock beside his bed. 3:11 AM. "<yawn> 's Friday mornin' Thursday, right?"

"Yes sir, Friday it is."

"Good, Suzie's Diner is open. I'm going to swing by and get a cup of coffee before I head in. Be there in 30 minutes."

Teddy had the all-night talk and news station playing on the radio during the drive to work. Talk radio was usually not his preference, but his headache wouldn't tolerate music this early in the morning. It was one of those call-in shows dedicated to insomniac UFO abductees and conspiracy theorists.

*"They're real, I tell you! I looked in his window last week and he had a coffin instead of a bed."*

*"Thanks for calling, Helen, but why were you looking in his window in the first place?"*

*"Well, he's so creepy, ain't he? Greasy hair, funny accent, says he's a professor. Has few visitors, just some creepy looking college kids. He only comes out at night and on rainy days, that's not normal!"*

*"I don't know Helen, sounds normal for college kids to me. Are you taking precautions?"*

*"Oh, yes. I have the garlic over the doorway, a wooden stake by the bedside, and my Ned had a priest come over and sprinkle the holy water just like it says on the website. Oh, and I only wear high-necked gowns."*

*"Very sensible Helen. Right after the break folks, we've got Bill in South Dakota who says his cat was replaced by aliens. Be right back."*

<beep> Dramatic music played for about 5 seconds, then a familiar recording came on...

*"Watch it in the evening, read about it in the morning, or Hear It Now on XVPR, News Talk for the Triad."*

*"This morning's top story, county health officials have ordered the recall of thousands of units of blood from area hospitals after discovering faulty storage units at the local blood bank. Three thousand homes in the Greene Park subdivision are still without power after last evening's thunderstorms, and area police are investigating a pair of suspicious deaths..."*

Teddy turned into the nearly empty parking lot, and switched off the car, silencing the news announcer in mid suspicion. He walked up to the front of the building and used his Faculty badge to unlock the security door. "Mike from Security" was on the phone at his desk and looked up in surprise.

"Oh, you're here already." he put down the phone. "I was just calling to tell you that John showed up about five minutes ago."

"He did? Did he say where he'd been?"

"Just muttered something about a migraine. He looked pretty pale."

"He always looks pale."

"Paler than normal. He looked pretty sick, to me. I told him you were coming in, but he said he'd take care of it."

"Okay. I'll go check on him then head back home for a few more hours' sleep."

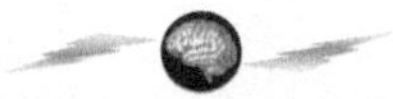

"It was just a breaker. He'd already reset it. So, I sent him home, told him not to come back until tomorrow. Then I checked the readouts on the other equipment and drove 20 minutes back home, only to get 2 hours sleep and be back here for the nine AM class. That's why I could do with another cup of your fine coffee, Jen."

Jeannette was leaning against the door frame of his office. "Get it yourself. Besides, you've got your own coffeepot."

"Yes, but I've only got a mild blend, too much acid otherwise. You have truly Wake-the-Dead coffee!"

"Flatterer! Did he say what it was?"

"He thinks it's either the flu or food poisoning."

"Really? I've got messages from Nigel and Keisha to their advisors saying pretty much the same thing. Either they had dinner together, or someone's been sharing germs!"

"Huh. Those three live in the lab, I can't see them getting into the sort of trouble you're implying."

"'Stranger things,' Doc. Nerd love is the finest."

"Get out of here. We both have work to do. Any word from Geoff or Emil? "

"Not yet, but then since you just taught the class you traded with Doctor Rose; I don't expect to hear from him until this afternoon. Doctor Tepes only interacts with me via email, and frankly, that suits me just fine."

"Yeah, I can understand that. Anything else?"

"Oh, right. I almost forgot. You need to approve the safety protocol transfer on the blood requisition."

Blood? As in blood banks? Why does that seem familiar?

"What, human blood? What am I requisitioning blood for?"

"It's for Doctor Tepes' stem cell cultures. You cosigned the protocol as the Department's representative to the Biosafety Committee, so you get to approve the transfers."

"FIFTEEN UNITS! Why the devil does he need fifteen units?"

"It's there on the protocol. The factor he's extracting is in nanomolar concentration and he needs a few micromoles to test on the cultures."

"Riiiight. But the original protocol stated 5 units each month. What's he doing? Drinking it?"

Teddy looked up at Jen. She tried to stifle a giggle, failed, and finally let it develop into full blown laughter. He just stared. She was getting short of breath from the laughter and gasped out: "Drinking it? <gasp> Vlad the Impaler? <laugh> Are you serious? <gasp> you're serious! <giggle> That is so funny!"

Teddy began to smile. "Yeah, now that you mention it. Maybe Vlad—I mean Emil, Geoff and the Night Crew students all got sick from drinking bad blood. Oh! Bad Blood. Yeah, I gotta write that down. Ha! Great title, great story idea."

Recovering her composure Jeanette gathered up the signed papers and quickly retreated from the office, the occasional giggle still escaping between deep breaths.

*Good thing I don't have any impending deadlines,* Teddy thought. Freshly inspired he brought up his short story on the word processor, erased the title and quickly rewrote the opening scene of his short story...

*BAD BLOOD, A SHORT STORY BY THEODORE EDWARDS*

*"VAN HELSING *NEVER* HAD TO DEAL WITH THIS," THOUGHT PROF. MARY SUE ROBBERTS, AUTHOR OF "BLOOD SCIENCE: THE MEDICAL TRUTH ABOUT VAMPIRES."*

*SHE LOOKED AROUND THE BLOOD BANK. "VAMPIRES? YOU THINK VAMPIRES DID THIS?" HER GLANCE TOOK IN THE BROKEN GLASS, OVERTURNED BOXES, EMPTY PLASTIC IV BAGS AND BLOOD SMEARED OVER EVERY SURFACE. SHE LOOKED AT THE POLICEMAN IN DISBELIEF. "HAVEN'T *ANY* OF YOU PEOPLE READ MY BOOK?"*

It was late afternoon when he wrote the closing scene:

*"SO, THEY CONTAMINATED THE BLOOD AND TRASHED THE BLOOD BANK TO FORCE THE VAMPIRES OUT IN THE OPEN?" ASKED INSPECTOR GORDON.*

*"YES, THE TWENTY-FIRST CENTURY IS OH SO CONVENIENT FOR THE MODERN VAMPIRE." PROF. ROBBERTS COULDN'T PASS UP THE CHANCE TO LECTURE. "FRESH BLOOD COMES IN CONVENIENT DISPOSABLE BAGS. NO HUNTING AND NO RISK OF CONTRACTING A RARE DISFIGURING DISEASE. NOT TO MENTION ALL OF THE INTOXICANTS AND DRUGS YOU FIND IN THE*

*BLOOD OF 'NUBILE MAIDENS' THESE DAYS. IT'S SO CIVILIZED, BUT WITH-OUT THE BLOOD BANK THEY HAD TO GET THEIR BLOOD THE OLD-FASH-IONED WAY."*

*"SO, THE TRAP WAS SET, AND NOW WE HAVE THREE LESS VAMPIRES IN TRIAD CITY. BUT WHO WERE THE HUNTERS?"*

*"WE MAY NEVER KNOW. AN ANCIENT ORDER, AT BEST GUESS. WE OWE THEM A DEBT OF GRATITUDE WHOEVER THEY ARE."*

*"WE OWE THEM A PLACE IN MY JAIL" GROWLED GORDON. "THERE'S NO ROOM FOR VIGILANTES IN TRIAD CITY."*

*"DON'T BE SO HARSH, INSPECTOR. AFTER ALL, YOU CALLED *ME* A VIGI-LANTE WHEN WE FIRST MET."*

*"AH, BUT YOU'RE THE PRETTIEST VIGILANTE I'D EVER MET." GORDON STOPPED, EMBARRASSED, AND STARED AT HIS FEET. AFTER A MOMENT HE CLEARED HIS THROAT. "AH, I DON'T SUPPOSE YOU'D CARE TO HAVE A CUP OF COFFEE?"*

*"WHY INSPECTOR! I NEVER THOUGHT YOU'D ASK!" ROBBERTS PUT HER ARM THROUGH GORDON'S AND STEERED HIM OUT THE DOOR. "I KNOW THIS GREAT LITTLE DINER THAT'S OPEN ALL NIGHT THURSDAY TO SUN-DAY..."*

Teddy breathed a sigh of relief, closed the file, opened an email window and quickly sent the manuscript off to Elise before he changed his mind and re-wrote the story for the third time.

There was an email from Jen. Doctor Rose had called in sick and asked if Teddy would post a note for the class and refer him to the review material on his website. Doctor Tepes would be in at six and thanked him for approving the transfer.

A notice popped up on his computer. Elise was online and wanted to talk about the story. Teddy opened the messenger client and began to type.

(17:41:13) Tedd09: Here.

Announcing yourself on the chat manager was usually polite. Announce then wait for a response. Elise came back almost immediately, she had been expecting him, after all, she had requested the dialog after he sent the manuscript.

(17:41:42) EllieWrites: There.

That was another custom of theirs. Teddy usually tried to start a conversation with a pun or joke. Fortunately, Elise usually got it and sometimes beat him to the punchline.

(17:42:18) EllieWrites: You named her MARY SUE?????

It was a bad joke about bad writers and fan fiction. "Mary Sue's" were thinly disguised versions of the writer him (or her)self.

(17:42:53) Tedd09: Sure, you kept telling me my characters were all Mary Sues

(17:43:26) Tedd09: and you bet I couldn't write seriously about vampires

(17:43:37) Tedd09: because I'm a scientist.

(17:43:48) Tedd09: So, I wrote logically,

(17:43:59) Tedd09: but not too seriously,

(17:45:21) Tedd09: and I named her Mary Sue.

It took a couple minutes for Elise's reply to come back.

(17:48:04) EllieWrites: LOL

(17:48:12) EllieWrites: You are a BAD man!

(17:48:39) EllieWrites: And I mean that in a nice way.

Teddy decided that deserved Elise's usual reply: 'LOL'—the email and messaging abbreviation for 'Laughing out Loud'.

(17:49:17) Tedd09:  LOL

After a few minutes without a return message, Teddy typed.

(17:56:34) Tedd09:  Gotta go.

(17:56:40) Tedd09:  Trish is waiting.

(17:56:47) Tedd09:  Tired

(17:56:53) Tedd09:  Didn't sleep well.

(17:57:05) Tedd09:  Tell you about it later.

(17:57:17) Tedd09:  'night.

Elise responded:

(17:57:43) EllieWrites:  Do.

(17:57:48) EllieWrites:  Tell.

(17:57:54) EllieWrites:  But later.

(17:58:06) EllieWrites:  get some rest

(17:58:21) EllieWrites:  Say Hi to Trish for me.

(17:58:40) EllieWrites:  'night.

They both signed off and Teddy shut down the programs he'd been using on the computer.  He was glad to have the story complete.  Once Elise had looked at it, he'd consider where to send it.  For now, he didn't want to even *think* about vampires and scientists.  Maybe his next story would be about lumberjacks or car mechanics.

As Teddy was packing up to go home, he saw John walk past his office door.

"I thought I told you to stay home."

"Sorry, Boss.  But I'm feeling much better, now.  Keisha gave me one of her herbal remedies."

"Herbal remedies from a Goth?  You trust it?"

"Naw, she's not like that.  She's a nice girl."

"I know, just kidding, but I heard she and Nigel were sick, too.  Back in my day that usually meant wild parties with illicit substances."

"Yes, yes, and you walked to class barefoot in the snow, uphill both ways.  It's not like that.  We were at a pizza place with other students.  Nigel, Keisha and I shared a pizza.  It must have been bad pepperoni."

"Okay.  Fine.  Just so you're well for Comps next week.  You've got your evening exam.  It seems that Pathology and Biochem have had to start doing the same thing.  Must be something in the water."

"Or in the blood."

"Huh?  What?  What was that?"

"Oh, nothing, just a night crew joke.  Don't worry.  I'll be ready."

"You'd better.  I lost one student early in my career to bad Comps.  Bright kid, couldn't take comprehensive exams worth a damn.  I hated to see him go."

"Don't worry about us so much, Doc.  We appreciate it, but we'll be fine.  I've gotta get downstairs and start testing the rats.  Mañana."

"Yeah. Tomorrow. No, tomorrow's Saturday. Give the rats the weekend off. Rest up, and study. Watch the 'Buffy' marathon on Sunday. 'See you Monday."

"Buffy? I'll pass. Nope, vampire hunters aren't for me. Too much blood."

"Oh sure, says the guy with fifteen units of blood in his fridge."

"What? How do you know about that?" John said, a bit too quickly.

"Well, I had to sign for it. Doctor Tepes will be looking for it. Compartment B-3. Tell him not to drink it all at once." Teddy turned and left the office, then called back over his shoulder. "Oh, and you've got some ketchup on your chin, you might want to wipe that off or people will be thinking *you* drank the blood!"

As he turned the corner and headed for the lobby, Teddy failed to notice the look of horror on John's face.

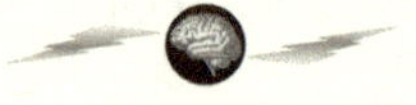

# HUNTER

*Authors note: Having shown her my urban fantasy story, my author friend promptly said "Okay, that's vampires, now, let's see werewolves, zombies, and ghosts. Well, the ghost story is in-process, and destined for another collection. The zombie story appears next, but the werewolf story was never actually finished prior to this volume. It was originally title "In the Blood," but that's too easily confused with the previous story, so I include it here as "Hunter."*

*I should also note that the events of this story were prompted by a news article from San Antonio about local high school kids joining "Werewolf Packs" and wearing ears and tails around after school. The parents were rather alarmed, but for the most part, it was passed off as just kids being kids.*

*But what if it wasn't?*

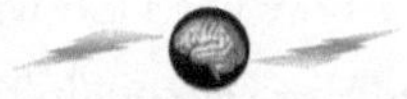

Shockey shaded his eyes as he looked out over the dusty fields at the rising sun. A slight mist formed as the air began to warm faster than the ground. As the morning progressed, the mist would be replaced with hazy waves of heat in the South Texas sun. It was early October, with cool nights and warm days, so the temperature would probably only get up to ninety-five.

There were small dots of green, and lots of scrub. It wasn't farmland, and was a bit sparse for cattle, but it suited Shockey just fine. He wanted privacy, and he had it...mostly.

With the warming of the day, he no longer needed the rough blanket he'd used to cover his legs through the night. So, he started folding it...and brushing off long white hairs.

"Dammit, Wolfie; you're shedding again. I gave you the bed and slept here in the chair, why do you need to get your damned hair all over my blanket?"

The sudden presence of hot, rancid breath on the back of his neck was enough to trigger any number of emergency reactions, but the wolfhunter ignored them, breathed deeply and continued speaking: "Wolfie, if you're going to be out in public, you need a bath, a flea dip and a breath mint." In a lightning-fast movement, he swung his right hand up and behind to cuff the white wolf on the side of the head, knocking it to the ground.

Without even looking at the stunned wolf, Shockey stood up, shook out the blanket, then folded it and took it inside the ranch house, Much like the fields outside, it was dusty, and bare. An old gas stove stood to the left; next to it was an ancient refrigerator with the cooling unit on top like a metal turban. In the middle was a small wooden table, and four mismatched metal chairs. On the right was a low bed, still made up, but with a wolf-sized depression in the middle, along with more white hairs. Above was a loft with another bed, but the wolf wouldn't climb the ladder, and Shockey couldn't be bothered. Sleeping in the rocker on the porch was enough.

"It's because you're warm, and he likes your smell," said a voice behind him.

Shockey turned to look at the man. He was tall, but with a light, muscular build. He looked like he was in his late twenties, maybe younger, given the absence of a visible beard. That was because his hair was nearly white; it didn't show on his face, and the hair on his head cut short, even if it *was* uneven.  The man clearly cut it himself without recourse to a mirror.

"If your wolf has been cuddling me in the middle of the night, Miles, you're going to have to find somewhere else to stay.  I'm not running a hotel."

"All evidence to the contrary.  Exactly *how* many horses, goats, chickens, and strays have you taken in over the years?"

"Animals, not wolves, Miles.  Besides, I'm back down to only two horses, and frankly, they're scared of your wolf."

"Yeah, well, he likes you, Bill."

"Unh-uh.  Not that name, please, I'm trying to let that one go."  There were several official documents hidden away in the house showing the name William Shockey, but considering that the date on the birth certificate and marriage license didn't match his apparent age, it was best if that name simply faded away.  Besides, he'd stopped being Bill after Lucy died.  She'd grown old, and Shockey...hadn't.

"Sorry, Hunter.  I should know better."

"Yes, you should!" Shockey waved at him with the coffee mug he'd picked up from the table after putting his folded blanket inside an open crate beside the bed. "It'll drive me to drink," he finished as he went over the refrigerator pulled out a gallon glass jar filled with clear brown liquid and poured some in the mug.

"That's tea."

"Mostly," Shockey countered, reaching for a small mason jar filled with clear liquid, and added a small amount to the tea. When Miles cocked an eyebrow at him, he said, "*I've* been awake all night. It's well past five for me."

Miles nodded, and said, simply, "full moon."

"Yup, found another one last night."

"Ah, that's what I smelled in the barn."

"Yes, and keep your wolf away from her.  She's freshly turned, and pretty confused."

"Softy."

"Well, we'll see. I'll need to see what kind she is, first. If she's *volkodlak*, I'll put her down myself, if *varulv*, I'll see if she can be fostered."

"As I said, you're a softy, Hunter.  C'mon, I'll go take a look with you."

Lying on the floor of the barn, whimpering, the creature looked innocuous. It was a black poodle—considerably larger than the 'standard size'—it would likely stand to nearly human height on its hind legs.  However, curled up on the dirt floor, it was more an object of pity than a feared werewolf, which was probably the reason Shockey had taken pity on her. "See?  She's just a baby."

When Miles didn't react, Shockey set down the mason jar he'd carried from the house, and bent down to look carefully at the Changed creature lying in front of him.  He reached out a hand, and the animal barely even registered his presence.  Historically a werewolf scratch or bite produced a lycanthrope with a wolf-like form, but ever since the Sixties, something strange had been rippling through the Lycan Community.  Shockey attributed it to the fact one could never tell in which 'recreational pharmaceuticals' a potential victim might have been indulging. These days, additional factors such as pet hair and dander affected The Change.  Shockey often found the new varieties of lycanthrope amusing, except for a few.  Were-chihuahuas were particularly vicious, and he had no pity for them.  Were-poodles, on the other hand, led a particularly difficult afterlife, and he felt sorry for them.  It gave a new meaning to the old Hunter saying about the problem being in the blood.

He noticed that the animal had one paw curled up.  Shockey was quite familiar with hooves and paws of all sorts, and immediately looked for anything out of place, quickly finding the shiny bit of metal embedded between the toes.  "Dang it, she's been pawing at my workbench."  He deftly removed the bit of silver and poured a small amount of liquid from the mason jar on the paw.  The poodle yelped and pulled its paw back, but soon got up and moved further back into the darkened barn.  The horses were out in the corral, so they weren't going to react to the dog-that-wasn't-a-dog, so he decided not to follow it.

Instead, Shockey looked out at the heat rippling off of the dusty fields and debated the merits of another cup of something cool to counter the building heat.

He returned to the house, walked over to the fridge and pulled out the two-gallon jar of tea he'd brewed in the sun the day before.

"Aren't you going to offer me some?" Miles asked.

Shockey just pointed to an old tin can with the cut edges of the lid filed off to allow drinking.  "Help yourself."

Miles grabbed the can, poured a small amount into it, swirled it to rinse the cup and then tossed it out the front door into the dirt.  He was just refilling the can when the phone rang.

The phone was an old black handset, and the ringer consisted of two bells mounted on the outside of the house at the corner of the porch.  That way Shockey could hear if someone called while he was in the barn.  Of course, he could always ignore it, and often did.  He could tell if it was important, since the caller would usually call back.

This was one of those times, so Miles put down his tin cup, walked over to the phone and answered it. "Shockey's." He stopped and listened. "Yes, Ma'am, I read about that, but I'm not the one you need to talk to.  I'm just Shockey's answering service." He held out the phone and grinned.

Shockey grimaced, but took the phone from Miles's hand. He put his hand tight over the microphone portion and whispered, "That's why I just let it ring." He took the hand away, held the handset up to his head and spoke into it. "This is Shockey."

He listened for a while and echoed Miles's earlier comment. "Yes, Ma'am.  I read about that."

After another pause, he continued. "No Ma'am, I think you have me confused with someone else. Hunter is my first name, not my occupation.  I offer farrier services." A small smile played at the edge of his mouth. "No Ma'am, that's *farrier* not furrier.  I shoe horses and provide minor veterinary services." He smiled broadly, relishing the confusion in the caller's voice as she tried to reconcile his words with his reputation. "No, Ma'am.  Thank you for calling, but unless they injure their paws, there's not much I can do.  Good bye." Shockey hung up the phone with a grin.  "Kids playing at being a wolf pack in high school.  Buncha furries, the lot of 'em." He squinted at the horizon.  It was still only a couple hours past dawn, but the nearly full moon had set. "Hmph. We're good for twelve hours, then.  Miles, I'm headed to town.  Are you coming?"

"Yeah, we going to check it out anyway?"

"Uh-huh. Lady was all concerned because her son was part of a 'werewolf pack' at school, just like the story in all the newspapers last week.  She heard from someone that I was a Hunter and wants me to do something about it.  Said I was 'Heaven Sent' or something like that." Shockey snorted as he edged past the young man to grab a shotgun and large-diameter, short-barreled rifle from the rack by the front door.  "Make yourself useful and grab a mag of tranks and the silver nitrate loads." He worked the slide of the shotgun with his left hand

and caught the ejected cartridge in his right hand.  Holding it up to the light he grunted, inspected the breech and the round poised to enter the chamber, then closed the action and thumbed the ejected round back into the magazine tube.

"The poodle going to be okay?"

"Most likely.  I imagine she's a confused girl at the moment.  There's water and protein bars in the barn. She'll be okay."

"Wait, protein bars for a newly turned were?  That's cruel."

"Naw, they smell and taste like meat.  She'll probably eat the whole bunch before we get back."

Shockey walked past the barn door on the way to his truck and yelled into the dark interior. "Miles and I are going to town.  There's clothes in the tack cabinet on the back wall.  Flip-flops, too, you're not going to want to wear shoes for a couple of days.  Food and water there as well.  Stay away from the workbench, there's silver there.  We should be back by moonrise, but if not, well, try to stick around.  I don't want to hunt you.

Shockey turned back to the pickup in time to see a white wolf leap in through the open passenger side window, then stick it's head back out with its tongue lolling.

"So, Wolfie's going, huh.  Ok, but stay on your side."

The pick-up truck used to be red, but was now faded and caked with South Texas dirt and dust.  Shockey put the rifle and shotgun on the rack mounted at the rear window; the box of 'special' tranquilizer darts was already on the front seat—on the driver's side.  Shockey put them under his seat and climbed up into the truck.  "Not going to call shotgun?" he asked, but received no answer.  "Yeah, I know, riding makes Miles nauseous, so I guess I'm talking to myself this trip."

They started down the gravel road from the ranch, kicking up more dust, but that was just a way of life.  It would take about ten minutes to get to a paved road, and another 15 before they'd start to see heavier traffic and building density as they approach the far outskirts of San Antonio. "I notice you haven't asked *why* we're going," Shockey began, determined to keep himself company, even if Miles wouldn't. The wolf growled, though, so he continued.

"Well, the kids are just teenaged furries, right? The article I read said that the kids organized an 'official' club at school so they would be allowed to wear tails and ears in class. Official club needs a teacher to be sponsor and advisor. It's the teacher we need to look at—a 'Mr. Fenris.'"

The wolf growled.

"Uh-huh. Raises my hackles, too."

Their first stop was a feed-and-seed store nestled in the eastern suburbs. The entire northeast part of the city had once been fields, farms, and quite a few stables. While most of that had grown into bedroom communities and boutique shops, this particular strip paralleling the railroad track had retained its farming and ranching heritage. After all, there had to be someplace to keep horses for the daughters of the military base commanders.

A bell jingled as Shockey walked into the shop. The bell rang a couple extra times as the door met an obstruction as it tried to swing shut behind him, then rang loudly as Wolfie shoved his nose into the glass and batted the door open again.

"Nice dog," the kid behind the counter told him. Then the kids face fell. "Aw, dammit. Now I'm going to have to clean the glass again."

"Wolf," Shockey said.

The kid looked at him quizzically. "Huh?"

"He's a wolf, not a dog."

"Oh. Uh, is he tame?"

"Not hardly, but he *is* housebroken."

The boy, whose nametag read 'Jerry' didn't seem to know how to respond, so Shockey continued. "Anyway, Jerry, I'm looking for Kurt. Is he in?"

"He's on the loading dock. We just got a truck in from Pure Milling. You can walk around..." He cut off as Shockey shook his head.

"I'll just go through the back."

Jerry moved to block his path to the door at the end of the counter, which elicited a growl from Wolfie. He looked scared, but held his ground. "Sir, I can't let you go through there."

Shockey stopped, smiled, and held up his hand. "Son, my name is Shockey. There's a note stuck to the side of your register there. You should read it.

Jerry tried to stay in front of the door while simultaneously reaching for the faded yellow piece of paper taped to the side of the register drawer. He barely managed to reach it, pulled it off, then glanced at the neat handwriting.

Jerry's eyes went wide. "Uh, s-sorry, s-sir. P-please go r-right back."

Shockey just smiled and followed the wolf through the door.

"Did you have to scare the clerk?" Miles asked.

"Aha! He speaks!"

"That doesn't answer the question, and of course I speak. You've warned me plenty of times about getting sick in your truck. You know, if you bought a new one, it wouldn't bounce as much, and I wouldn't get nauseous."

"And you like the wind in your face."

"And yes, I like the wind in my face, it helps with the nausea."

"I'm still going to make you pick all of the wolf hairs out of the upholstery."

"It's solid vinyl, I could wash it out with a hose."

"But then you'd short out my radio."

"Which you *never use,* you old fossil."

"I like the quiet."

"Which is why you always talk to me even when you know I can't answer?"

"Well, at least you don't talk back!"

"Shockey! You never change, do you?  Still arguing with Miles." The store owner, Kurt, gently placed a bag of feed on the pallet.  He handled it effortlessly, but from the size, had to be either 50 or 100 pounds.

"Would you want me to?  Change, I mean."

"Naw, don't ever change Bi—uh, sorry, Hunter." Kurt turned back to unloading the truck, grabbing another large bag of horse feed and adding it to his stack. "What about you, Miles? Doing okay?  Your wolf behaving?"

"Okay, and yeah, pretty much."

"No, he's not, he claimed the bed.  I'm sleeping in a chair most of the time," Shockey corrected.

"You've got another bed in the loft, not to mention all that soft hay in the barn. Why don't you sleep there instead of a chair?" Kurt asked, motioning to one of his staff to remove the full pallet and replace it with an empty so that he could continue unloading the shipment.

"He's got a stray in the barn."

"Stray what, cat? Calf? Goat?"

Shockey said nothing, but emitted a faint sound like a deep-throated growl.  He looked meaningfully in the direction of the teenage boy operating the powered pallet lifter.

Kurt glanced in that direction, then back to Shockey and smiled.  "Oh, don't worry about him.  Miguel is one of mine.

"Damn, you both just can't help yourself, always taking in strays," Miles muttered under his breath.

Kurt certainly heard it, though, because his eyes briefly turned yellow, then back to normal, but with a slight twinkle. "Ah, so.  Not sleeping at all, then.  You're watching to see if he turns."

"Nope.  She.  Already turned. Watching to see what kind."

"Oho!  Let me guess.  Poodle, black hair.  Stands about yay tall?" Kurt held his hand at waist-height.

"You know her?"

"Oh yes, or at least Miguel does." He turned and shouted to the boy who had just moved the full pallet of seed into a storage spot on the far wall of the stockroom. "HEY MIGGY!  Shockey found Faye!"

The boy looked up, turned to face Kurt, and his face lit up.  He ran over to them and breathlessly and looked at Shockey with a hopeful expression.  "You found her?  She's okay?"

"Remains to be seen, son.  What do you know of her Change?"

The boy looked down, somewhat embarrassed. "It's a silly club at school.  They call themselves The Wolf Pack."

Shockey and Miles turned to look at each other, then turned back. The motion was not lost on Kurt, who prompted the boy to continue. "Go on. Is there a Senior Lycan prompting this?"

"Oh no, they don't actually know anything about the Change. The club does silly stuff like wear fake ears, hang furry tails off their belts, smearing themselves with a smelly ointment, wearing a cape made from a wolf skin…"

"Wait, hold up, there. You've seen this skin?" Miles asked.

"Yeah, it's in pretty bad shape, it looks more like a coyote, than a wolf, though."

"Yeah, that fits, kinda," Miles responded.

"Anyway, the kids do dumb stuff like that. Last summer, when the full moon fell on Wednesday, they all slept outside, uncovered, moon on their face. They were all drinking this really bad-tasting beer and chanting in some language. Faye started to act a bit weird after that. She told about it, and admitted she was kind of scared because she had strange dreams that night. Then she dropped out of school last month."

"When last month?" Kurt prompted.

"About when you'd think. Last full moon. At least, that's my supposition. I saw her once, in the daylight back then, and she was complaining about her poodle shedding—but poodles don't shed. There've been reports of a stray poodle in the neighborhood, but rumor is her parents think she ran off to Houston to live with someone."

"Sounds like someone stumbled upon the old rituals," Shockey said.

Kurt thanked Miguel, told him to head to the office and write down all of her particulars, address, parents names, phone numbers, what school she attends, names of close friends, etc. When the stock boy was out of earshot—real earshot, further than most lycans can hear, that is—Kurt turned back to

Shockey and Miles. "That's exactly what it sounds like. Almost like my ancestors did."

"Technically, you were summoned, not turned, *Kurtadam*. You're also a guardian."

"Explains why he takes in strays, but it doesn't explain you, Shockey," Miles said. "So, which ritual?  It's not the coyote skin, I can tell you that."

"Oh, is that true...*Ma'ii*?" Shockey asked Miles with a grin.

"The damn Navaho said I looked as scrawny as a starving coyote, and the name stuck. Don't give me that, *Seth*."

The skies had been getting darker, and a bright flash of lightning, and immediate peal of thunder interrupted the discussion. "Um, yeah.  Names have power. Maybe we should stop.  I'm sorry, Shockey," Miles said, contritely.

"Apology accepted, Miles. So, back to 'Faye,' if she turned last month, and we haven't heard about unexplained human or animal attacks, she's probably not *volkodlak*."

"You're thinking she's *varulv*?" Kurt asked?

"It would fit, the rituals the kids were attempting sound Norse. Besides she was pretty quiet last night."

"She had a sliver of *silver* in her paw, old man! Or did you do that deliberately?"

"No, not me, but I'm thinking she didn't get it from my workbench, either."

"An amateur hunter?"

"You know the old question.  'What's worse than a rampaging werewolf?'"

"'The incompetent hunter who chases it.'" Kurt and Miles answered in unison.

"Right.  Let's get that info from Miguel and go check out her neighborhood. Oh, and Miles—shake the loose wolf hair off before you get back in the truck."

Faye Oliver lived in a part of town that had been trendy, once, then succumbed to the inevitable aging of its residents.  After going through a phase where the homeowners were predominately retirees, if had once again become popular with young families, if not as *rich* as it once was.  The streets were lined with comfortable ranch-style, one-story homes.  Yards were mostly enclosed with six-foot wood fencing, and each house had at least one large tree that was clearly older than fifty years. Many of the two-car attached garages were remodeled into additional space, and all but a few of the once-prevalent backyard swimming pools had been filled-in.

The house was red brick, with an oversized carport in front of a remodeled garage.  Faye's parents weren't willing to receive visitors inside, but had no problem setting up folding chairs and serving cold lemonade outside under the carport.

"Oh, Faye left last month to go visit her cousin Jamie in Houston," Mrs. Oliver was telling Shockey. "Those two were always thick as thieves. They'd run off and get into trouble for a week or two, then they'd head home and get back to school with very little loss."

"They would... miss school? Regularly?" Shockey asked, incredulously.

"Oh yes, Faye's just such a phenomenal student, she can skip over a whole bunch of classes, show up, take the test, and pass at the top of her class.  I mean, even right now, she's ranked third in her class of twelve-hundred students."

"I asked her why she wasn't first, but she just told me she didn't want the pressure," her father added.

"You're sure she's not just telling you that?" Miles had an eyebrow raised, doing his best Spock imitation.

"Oh, certainly, Principal Reyes and I golf together every month. He's been singing her praises, especially since her performance at the gifted student camps the past few summers," Mr. Oliver assured them.

"Is she involved in many extracurricular activities?"

"Oh, yes, she just loves her clubs and activities. Band, choir, math team, drama, robotics..."

"Has she ever mentioned something called a Wolf Pack?" Shockey asked.

"I think they call that 'Cosplay,'" Miles interjected.

"Oh, no, I don't think so." Mr. Oliver looked thoughtful as he shook his head.

"Nope, not at all. I heard about those silly children and their fluffy ears and tails, but no, Faye wouldn't do anything as frivolous as that," Mrs. Oliver said with certainty.

"But you just said she runs off and skips school for days, maybe weeks at a time. How is that different?"

"Oh dear no. That's *artistic*!"

The conversation didn't seem to be getting anywhere. They certainly weren't getting any impression that Faye's parents thought she was in danger, or involved with a group that would attempt dangerous lycanthrope transformation rituals. Shockey and Miles thanked the Oliver's and rose to go, but Mrs. Oliver surprised them with an afterthought.

"I do wish she would call, soon, the faculty advisor from the summer camp was trying to get in touch with her."

"Oh, really? What did Mr. Fenton want?" Mr. Oliver asked his wife.

"He didn't say, or rather, he just said he was calling to see how she was doing. Oh, and it's not Fenton, it's Fenris, dear."

Shockey and Miles shared a look of surprise.

Shockey and Miles were both so distracted as they got back in the truck, that neither spoke for several minutes after they pulled away from the house.

"Fenris again," Miles said.

The shock of Miles' voice in the moving truck startled Shockey so much that he slammed on the brakes right in the middle of a moderately busy street.

"Miles?"

"Uh?" Miles looked at Shockey, who dipped his chin while looking at the man in the passenger seat.

Miles looked down, caught view of his stomach and legs, and just shrugged. "So?"

"What about your motion sickness?"

"My stomach's already churning.  I think I might know this Fenris."

"Norse mythology."

"Yeah, but he's not Norse.  He's Arcadian, from the Peloponnese—Greece."

"Ah, from Pliny the Elder: 'A man of Arcadia, once per year, chosen from the Anthus clan, destined to spend nine years as a wolf.' But wasn't he supposed to turn human again if he refrained from eating human flesh?"

"Yes, but Anthus—that's actually *his* name, not the clan name—developed a taste for flesh, anyway. He would resist for a time, then he claimed that the smell got to him. He'd break down and have a meal, usually an indigent, and spend the next nine years as a wolf. He'd turn back, and try to live a normal life until the cravings started again."

"That doesn't explain the Wolf Packs and involvement with school kids, though."

"No, that came later. He believed that if he ate someone immediately after The Change, he'd break the curse, but the person had to *want* the Change."

"Ah, thus school kids experimenting with Norse summoning rituals."

"Last I saw him, he'd been experimenting with the Slavic rituals, not Norse, but the risk of getting *volkodlak* are too great. I threatened to end him, but a pesky war got in the way."

"War? Which one, Peloponnesian?"

Miles snorted, and smacked Shockey on the shoulder with the back of his hand.

"Fourth Crusade."

The two decided it was time to visit Mrs. Rodriguez, the woman who'd called that morning. It was getting late in the day, though, and Miles asked a question that had been nagging at Shockey.

"Is Faye going to be okay?"

Shockey grunted and pulled out his cell phone, flipped it open and pressed a bunch with an audible 'click.'

"A *flip-phone*?  Are you planning on joining the twenty-first century before it's over, man?"

"Hush." Shockey said to Miles, then back to the phone.

"Kurt?  Yeah, Shockey.

"Your boy, there, Miguel? He have a Cert?

"He does, great.  Have him pick up some food and head out to my place

"Yes, human food.

"Of course not.  When have I ever locked anything?

"Good, thanks,  He's got about two hours until sunset, and moonrise will lead that by five minutes, so he needs to be careful.

"No, I'm not expecting that, in fact, that's why I sending him. But he's not to let anyone else near her.

"Yes, that does help, but also tell him there's a loaded shotgun just inside the front door of the house.

"Good for him.  Tell him it's just in case, though.

"Right. Thanks. We're onto something and Miles thinks he knows what's going on. I'll call you later. 'bye"

Shockey flipped the phone closed as they pulled into a neighborhood about ten miles northeast of the Oliver's. Despite the relatively short distance, it had taken nearly an hour to make their way through the rush hour traffic.

The Rodriguez family was eating supper when Shockey knocked on their door. It was a newer neighborhood—bigger houses, bigger yards, bigger piles of money needed to maintain the lifestyle.

Despite the urgency of his wife's early call, Mr. Rodriquez insisted that all discussion wait until the family had a chance to complete their evening meal. Shockey and Miles waited in the truck, anxiously watching the clock.

Finally, Mrs. Rodriguez came back to the door and motioned the men to come in...but they soon learned that their son, Julio, had already left for a "Scout meeting." When asked where the club was meeting, they were told that Julio had volunteered a piece of property his family was developing north of town on the edge of Canyon Lake. The boys in Julio's troop often camped and picnicked there.

"We're building a retirement home there, but so far, we've only put in a barn and a boathouse. The Scouts like to camp, swim, and occasionally Julio's father takes them out water skiing."

"It will be dark in an hour, and it takes thirty minutes to get there from here," Miles cautioned.

"Understood," Shockey answered him. "Missus Rodriguez? Ma'am, could you draw a map so that we can find your property easily?  I'm sure the boys will be fine, but it would be a good idea to talk with Julio, and we don't want it to be dark by the time we find him."

"Oh, my, yes, but I can take you there. Just let me get my keys and you can follow me. Hugo!" she called over her shoulder, "I'm showing Mister Hunter up to the lake house.  Be back soon."

The only response was a grunt from the living room, barely audible over the sound of the evening news.  Miles had already gone to the truck, and Shockey followed once Mrs. Rodriguez had usher him out and gone toward the garage.

A late model luxury car pulled out of the driveway and headed down the road. Shockey had to hurry to keep up. "Just as I always thought, those cars only have two speeds—slow as molasses and *bat-out-of-hell*!"

When there was no response from Miles, Shockey turned to see the white wolf with it's head out the window.

"So, nausea? Tracking? Or just sniffing the neighborhood?"

The wolf just growled.

"Right. Tracking it is."

With no traffic, the drive to Canyon Lake was just over thirty minutes. On a Friday evening, with families heading to the lake for the weekend, it could often take an hour—or more when one included winding through the recent growth of lakeside communities. Following Mrs. Rodriguez was an experience, though. Her driving would put a NASCAR driver to shame, and it took exactly twenty-five minutes until they were pulling into a large wooded lot with a large cleared area on a rise overlooking the water.

Several tents were set up in the clearing, as well as sleeping bags and pads laid out in the open. The night would be clear, so sleeping in the open was an option, Shockey supposed. Still, the temperatures were forecast to drop fairly low—for South Texas—that is, so the fact that the bedrolls were already laid out was unusual.

There was a large barn off to one side, nearly nestled in the trees. By the water was a dock and a two-story building large enough to hold a couple of boats, with a small living area on a second story. There were some teenagers on the dock, as well as several surrounding a firepit by the waterside.

Wolfie jumped out the open window, and headed for the trees to scout the area as Shockey got out of the truck. Mrs. Rodriguez also got out of her car and came over to talk to him.

"Oh, what a beautiful dog you have, Mister Hunter. I'm surprised I didn't see him—her?—at the house.  Oh, and where's your friend, Mister Miles?"

Shockey decided not to correct her regarding names or Wolfie's taxonomy.  After all, it was...complicated. "Actually, Miles is running an errand for me..." *True.* "...and Wolfie's a bit shy. He needs to go take care of business after a ride." *Partially true.* "He'll come back in a minute." *Not...necessarily true.* "But...are those scouts from your son's troop?"

Mrs. Rodriguez looked at the mixed group of teenaged boys and girls...some of whom appeared to be wearing fuzzy clothing. "Why, no, that's not the Scouts at all! That looks like some of Julio's friends from school!"

She pointed to an older adult standing over the firepit. "And that's that creepy Mister Fenris. Why, I have half-a-mind to just go right over there and give him a piece of my mind!"

"Ah, Ma'am, it's probably best if you don't do that.  Leave this to me." He showed her a small folding case, and something inside flashed brightly in the setting sun. "Although, if you could call the Comal County Sheriff and ask for Sheriff Douglas, I'd be much obliged. Tell him Shockey called, and give him this address.  Now, you should probably stay in your car, or even head back home to your husband."

The woman looked at his suspiciously. "This sounds like you're expecting trouble, Mister Hunter.  I'll have you know I have my Concealed Carry Permit!  I'm not leaving without my Julio, and without him, these people are all trespassing." She reached into her handbag and pulled out a firearm that was way too heavy for her to use reliably, although she did seem to be handling it correctly, so he could be wrong.

"Thank you, Missus Rodriguez, but for now, all I want to do is talk to Mr. Fenris.  I'll send Julio and the kids over, and you can keep them safe until the sheriff or his deputies arrive."

"Very well, but I *will* protect my Julio!"

"Yes, Ma'am. I'm sure you will."

Shockey saw the flash of white circling through the tress down toward the water. It was surprising how well a white wolf could hide in plain sight, so the fact that he could see Wolfie meant that he was *intended* to be seen.

Good. Wolfie was getting into place. Shockey started walking toward the group by the firepit.

"Hey, man, this is private property. It's my family's land." A young man from the dock-side group started in his direction. "You need to leave or I'll call the cops."

"You must be Julio. Your mom's over there and wants to talk with you. Besides, I *am*...well, not a cop, but I am in *enforcement*."

"Mom? She's..." As he walked up from the water, he could see past the slight hill to the driveway. "Nononono! She can't *be* here! She'll mess everything up! Mr. Fenris says we can't have any unbelievers here!"

"Yes, and that's why I need to speak with your Mister Fenris."

"He won't talk to you. He's started his meditation."

"Oh, he'll talk to me. Now, you'd best go talk to your mom."

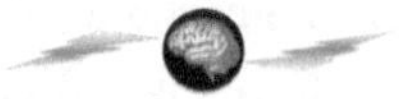

The kids by the firepit seemed engrossed in their activities. Several were applying ointment to their skin; others were tying furred skins to their arms and legs. Fenris appeared to be muttering to himself and oblivious to everything until Shockey approached within ten feet.

The man turned, and his eyes blazed yellow as he shifted—his face becoming elongated, his body becoming more angular, with longer limbs and claws on his fingers.  His voice came out in a growl. "Begone, Mortal!  You have no place here."

Shockey smiled to himself.  *Yup, Werewolf.*  He checked his watch. *Moonrise. Not Anthus, then. Not volkodlak, either, or he would've been rampaging instead of corrupting kids.*

"Sorry buddy, not mortal. My name's Hunter Shockey.  What's yours?"

"I don't have to tell you, mortal, but the children call me Fenris."

"Nope, once again, I knew **Fenris**. You ain't him. As I said, I'm not mortal."

"Ah, a wolfhunter.  How quaint.  I have killed many of your kind."

"Oh, I doubt you've met *any* of my kind.  After all, you're still here."

"Pfaw, you and the other blood traitors are all alike.  My children will eliminate the others."

"So, that's your plan?  These kids are to be your minions? You plan to make them slaves?"

"No, they will take the place of my slaughtered sons, and we shall rule!"

Shockey checked out of the corner of his eye. Wolfie wasn't in view, but he could tell the wolf was there.  The kids were absolutely still.  Their eyes glowed slightly, and they seemed to be in thrall to Fenris.

"Slaughtered sons?  Oh, do tell me more. What is your name?"

"I do not have to tell you anything, mort—"

Shockey's eyes glowed red, and a bright flash of light emanated from his body. "TELL ME YOUR NAME! I *compel* you!"

The werewolf wobbled, as if struck by a great force. His eyes went wide and reflected a red-gold glow as he stared at Shockey. "I am Lycaon. Who—who are you?" There was fear in his voice now.

"You would know me as Seth."

"You might want to tell him the rest," a voice growled from behind Lycaon. Miles stood there in his hybrid form, part giant white wolf, part tall lanky human.

"Sure; just call me Seth Adamson."

Lycaon threw his head back and laughed. "Seth, son of Adam, you think you can scare me and compel me? I was created by *Zeus*!"

"Okay, but you should know that Miles here was created by *me*," Shockey told him as Miles shifted back into his white wolf form and leapt at Lycaon."

The park police finished up with the kids as Shockey and the deputy watched the doors close on the ambulance. Lycaon had shifted back to human form on death, and *most* of the wounds and scars had disappeared with the shift. Now, he looked like an ashen-faced, forty-ish man of Mediterranean descent. He had the short curly hair often associated with Greek sculpture. "Mister Fenris" had been an earlier victim of Lycaon, and this man looked nothing like the teacher.

"He's not going to give my coroner a heart attack by waking up on the slab, is he?"

"Nope, that's why you're sending him down to my office in San Antonio," Shockey told him holding out his Ranger badge, a silver five-pointed star inside a hollowed-out circle. It was real silver, too, making it as good as any weapon or religious symbol for dangerous Lycans. He was careful never to show the back, though, since the name "Hayes" and date—1840—might cause someone to accuse him of stealing an artifact. He'd done a little work to ensure that it looked new enough to be considered "classic," but not "ancient," and had it mounted in a nice new leather wallet to keep unwanted eyes away from his past.

Shockey laughed to himself at the irony. Lycaon was the one for whom all of were-kind were named: Lycaon—Lycanthrope. Actually, silver would not have affected the ancient Arcadian king, but he was no match for an even older Guardian Wolf.

"Okay, I'm cleaned up enough that the medics aren't going to want to check me out," Miles said from his side.

"Ah, but I need your statement..." the deputy began, then stopped as Shockey's eyes glowed faintly red. "...or not."

Julio and his schoolmates were free to go; many of them reported being woozy and unclear. It helped that nobody could clearly remember seeing what happened—even Mrs. Rodriguez. The park police suspected drugs or booze, but were unable to find any evidence of that. They'd even brought along a device to look underneath the water at the edge of the lake, but again, there was nothing to find that hadn't been there for years.

Of course, the animal skins and various ointments and potions were long gone. Shockey had gathered it all into a single pile on the firepit, blew out a breath, and it all went up in a brief burst of flame. The remains were now indistinguishable from the rest of the ash from the campfire.

As the kids began to depart in their vehicles, the park police and sheriff's officers began to disperse. Sheriff Douglas had sent only "experienced" officers, and Shockey appreciated their discretion. He had only needed to identify himself to the senior-most deputy to allay their concerns for his own actions. After all, he and Douglas had dealt with a *chupacabra* a few months earlier, and had a standing arrangement for dealing with the constant influx of *alux*—the

Mexican version of imps and gremlins. When Texans complained about the "leaky" Mexican border, they didn't know the half of it; the immigration issue was nothing compared to the influx of supernatural creatures accompanying them.

Once the last officer was finished with interviewing her, Mrs. Ramirez let go of her son long enough to approach. "Oh, Mister Hunter. You are a *SAINT*; I don't know *what* we would have done if you hadn't been here. That awful man. The officer says he must have been on drugs. It's no wonder he had a heart attack!"

"Yes, Ma'am, that's what I've heard. It's all in the blood, they say."

"Anyway, you must be our guardian angel *or something*, to have been here at just the right time."

"Yes, Ma'am, if you say so, Ma'am. But frankly, I'm no angel." Shockey smiled when he said it though, both to diffuse the situation, and at the obvious confusion on her face. He looked over at the deputy and saw amusement at the exchange. "Are we free to go?" he asked, and the officer nodded. He bid farewell to Mrs. Rodriguez, promising to drop by for dinner sometime.

Miles was waiting in the truck when Shockey got there. "Not going to shift for the ride?"

"Oh, I plan to. You know I prefer the wind in my face, it keeps my stomach from getting upset. I needed to show you this first." He held out his phone; the screen showed a picture of a poodle and German shepherd curled up together on a pile of hay. Items in the background identified the location as Shockey's barn.

"Who took the picture?"

"Kurt. He went out to the farm to check on Miguel."

"Well, he seems to have a girlfriend. Can't say I disapprove, Kurt's good to those he fosters." Shockey paused a moment, then continued, "but a *German* shepherd named *Miguel*?"

"There's German settlements in Texas! Fredericksburg, New Braunfels, Shulenburg, Boerne..."

"Okay, Okay. I get it. Now don't shift when the truck is moving. I don't want the wind blowing your hair and dander on me."

Miles said nothing; just grinned back at him and turned his face toward the window.

Shockey pulled out onto the road leading east, he wanted to circle around San Antonio and avoid the city on the way back to the ranch. He reached into his shirt pocket and pulled out a small, irregular cigar, held it up and looked at it, then blew gently at it. Flame touched the tip of the tobacco and it quickly turned to gray ash. Putting the cigar in his mouth, he drew on it to produce a bright red coal, and spoke to Miles without looking away from the road. "Nope, as I told the lady, '*I ain't no saint, and I ain't no angel.*' It might also be time for a new name. I can take a few years off my face like you always do and create a new identity. What do you think of 'Seth Hunter?'"

He turned to look at Miles, and saw the white wolf looking back. With open jaw and lolling tongue, it looked for all the world like the wolf was laughing at him.

"Yeah. Me, too." Shockey laughed back.

# NEURAL ALCHEMIST

*Authors note: I'm quite proud of this story, it's the one that truly defined my start in writing science fiction.  It's also the only story in this collection to have been previously published—in the 2017 book Science Fiction by Scientists. It also boasts my favorite opening.*

*Once more, this story is a response to my friend's challenge, to write a vampire, ghost, zombie, and werewolf story and stop writing strictly hard SF featuring scientists.*

*Right.*

*It may be fantasy, but it still features a scientist and university setting.*

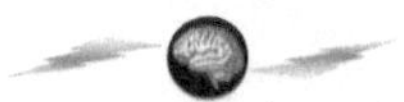

MOVIES AND TV SHOWED THE ZOMBIE APOCALYPSE AS A SINGLE EVENT, OCCURRING SUDDENLY DUE TO AN UNCONTROLLED INFECTION OR SOME MYSTERIOUS, MYSTICAL EVENT.  THAT COULDN'T HAVE BEEN FARTHER FROM THE TRUTH. IT STARTED SLOWLY, SUBTLY, AND WE JUST CHALKED IT UP TO OUR OWN BURGEONING MEDICAL AND TECHNOLOGICAL ADVANCE-MENTS: A FEW LESS PATIENTS DIED, ACCIDENT VICTIMS RECOVERED, ONCE

DEADLY DISEASES BECAME LESS SO. THE FIRST WORLD WAS CAUGHT UP IN HUBRIS AND WE PATTED OURSELVES ON THE BACK FOR BEING SUCCESSFUL AT CHEATING DEATH. NO ONE PAID MUCH ATTENTION TO THE FACT THAT IT WAS HAPPENING IN THE REST OF THE WORLD, TOO. THE HOWLING MOBS AND RAVAGING HORDES WOULD COME LATER... MUCH LATER.

The office walls were a cool, professional blue designed to send the message that this was an office of authority. The University logo dominated the wall behind the receptionist's desk. The occupant of that desk did her best to ignore the man sitting in one of the visitor chairs. Her aura of professional detachment was marred by the furtive glances whenever she thought he wasn't looking.

Somewhere a battery-operated clock ticked loudly in the silence. From an adjacent office could be heard the clicking of keys on a computer.

Professor John Wissen sat waiting.

He has neither comfortable nor uncomfortable. None of that mattered anymore. Nevertheless, he sat.

Waiting.

As if he had all the time in the world.

Tick.

The telephone ring was jarring in the near silence of the waiting area. Wissen did not react. Alarm or boredom; neither mattered. The receptionist, however, practically leapt out of her ergonomic chair to answer the phone. After a brief "Hello" and a moment of listening, she hung up the phone, turned to the visitor and said: "The Associate Dean will see you now, Professor Wissen. Please, go right in."

She gestured vaguely in the direction of an interior door, and turned back to her computer screen with a visible sigh of relief when he complied.

This office was a distinct contrast to the waiting area, warm beige walls, richly toned wooden furniture, pictures of family members, personal mementoes. The surroundings perfectly suited Associate Dean Laura Diaz.  Well-regarded by faculty and administration alike, she had pursued Wissen's case with the administration.

She stood and came out from behind her desk to greet Wissen, shaking his hand—one of the few to still do so.

"Sit, John." She gestured to one of a pair of comfortable chairs, taking the other herself.

"Thank, you, Dean." Wissen said, formally, as he sat. "I appreciate the awkward position this has put you in."

"Nonsense, John." She smiled at him, a heartwarming, genuine smile, not like the furtive glances he'd been receiving lately.  "Why so formal?  You've called me Laura since we were graduate students."

"Sorry, I just figured with recent events you might need to keep some detachment."

"No, the Board of Trustees specifically asked me to work on this <u>because</u> they know we are such old friends."

"Oh.  Thanks.  I do appreciate it, really." Wissen tried to smile.  It wasn't easy. First he had to identify the facial nerve and send it a signal to contract first the cheek muscles, then mandibular muscles and then the skin around the eyes.

Diaz laughed. "John, if you only knew how silly that looks! You are the only person I know that smiles one muscle at a time."

"Technically I'm not a person any more, Laura." Wissen's face fell back into its habitual, neutral expression.

"Well, about that," Diaz continued, "The Faculty Executive Council decided on "Professor Emeritus" since they didn't think that the Board would go for "Professor Posthumous." In fact, the Board agreed, but then they sent the whole thing over to Legal. Once the lawyers work it out, the Board will give final approval." She paused and took a deep breath. "Sooooo... I just got off the phone with Legal. They're having to get pretty inventive, given that there's really no precedent for your situation."

"But they will allow me to continue working?"

"Oh, yes, that was established first, it's the reason for the official position. A liability issue, I was told, if you don't have an official appointment, you can't be here. Your salary, on the other hand..."

"I suppose that means they can still only pay my estate?"

"No, Legal says we can put it in something like a Living Trust, where life partners put all of their assets into a secured fund, but can spend it at need."

"So, I get an Unliving Trust?" Wissen asked, just the sides of his mouth pulled up in another attempt at a smile.

"I suppose we could call it that. Your son will still be the trustee and beneficiary, but you will have unlimited rights at the funds. Legal also says we should pay your apartment and bills from it and register your car to the trust. They've gotten approval to roll your IRA and 403c retirement funds into it as well." Diaz paused and frowned. "The insurance company, though, insists that they won't pay off the life insurance."

"Screw 'em. Tell Legal that if they won't pay Life, then they have to pay Permanent Disability. After all, I *did* die in a covered automobile accident." Wissen's bitter tone belied the blank look on his face.

Diaz laughed. "Actually, Legal told *me* that they could probably get that. If they don't go for a lump-sum payment, it could even cost them more than paying out the life insurance."

Wissen sat in silence for a moment. "But how can Bill administer a trust here? He's in Japan for the next three years."

"Ah, well that's where Legal started getting inventive!" Diaz reached over to her desk and picked up a folded letter. "Here is Bill's designation of a 'memorial gift' to the University. Thanks to his own job and savings, he doesn't feel he needs the inheritance, at least not now. He has authorized us to draw half of the trust as an endowment under the institution's control. He included anything of which he was a beneficiary, such as the royalties on your patents and your retirement funds." She paused. "By the way, what did you do, pour all of Kath's estate into your retirement accounts?"

"No, actually, most of it went to Bill. It's just that I always contributed the maximum legal amount. It adds up."

"Oh, so that's what it was. I wish my retirement had done as well. Well, with this and the fact that the University still holds your NIH and DoD grants, the Board *had* to reconfirm your faculty appointment and give you back your lab."

"I will *so* enjoy getting out of the basement." Wissen tried again to smile, but he wasn't up to sarcastic yet. The past three months of losing his lab, equipment and students, not to mention car and apartment while living on a cot in one of the antiquated basement labs had worn thin.

"There's still a catch." Diaz reminded him.

"Yeah, I know. I'm still dead."

"Yes, that's true, but I mean your legal identity. Trust aside, you don't legally exist: you can't own property, be paid or enter a contract. The trust will take care of that, but the real issue is identification. You technically can't drive, even though the DMV won't press the issue until your license is due in three years. But you have no *official* status, no ID, no passport, no Social Security number."

"No Social Security, no taxes, no withholding. That doesn't sound so bad."

"No leaving the country, no air travel, no getting stopped by the police, because if you get asked for ID, it comes back as stolen."

"Oh, not so hot then."

"There's one way out, though. If you are right that this is a result of something in the lab, then it's patentable."

"WHAT? You can NOT patent a person."

"Well, technically you're not a person, and we can patent a cell culture, and you are most definitely a unique cell culture line. Industry Relations has already filed the provisional patent. They just need your notebooks to finalize it."

"DAMN it, Laura, I am not a cell culture!"

"At least it would give you a legal identity."

"Sure, it does: 'Property of the University'. Are they going to send Dexter to put a property tag on me? Make me wear it on my forehead, tattoo it on my rump, or just notch my ears like a lab rat?"

"John, it's the only way."

"Sure, Laura, I know. This whole situation is hard; I just never imagined that anything could be worse than negotiating a DoD contract, but this certainly looks that way." He stood up, slowly, and attempted the smile again. "But at least it is something. Thank you Laura."She also stood, and took his hands briefly, before turning to the office door. "I know it is hard, John, but just look at where you are. We'll make this work."

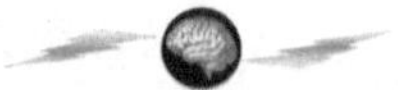

The lecture hall normally seated 125 students; this class had no more than 75 in attendance. Classroom dynamics tempered by medical student politics would usually result in the front two rows being completely filled, with the rest of the rows only partially filled—except for the back row which always hosted the same few students. Today the students were about half in front and half in back. There were only two vacant seats in the back row.

*Morbid curiosity or morbid fear?* Wissen thought to himself. The bodies in the back row... *Okay, that was a morbid thought...*, the STUDENTS in the back row, plus the unusual proliferation of extra recording devices per student probably accounted for the calls the Dean's office had received demanding that "The Abomination" be removed from the Faculty.

Just outside the lecture hall was a flyer announcing the special lecture. Some wit had defaced it, crossing out Wissen's name, and replacing it with that of the ghost professor from those young wizard books written a few years back. What was the story? Oh, yes, the old wizard professor had died in mid-lecture and kept on lecturing as a ghost without noticing. Not quite the same, but he supposed there were worse names to be stuck with.

The buzz of voices started to die down. John just sat and waited for his introduction. He was just gratified that any students showed up. There had been a protest piece in the newspaper last week—it was written by the local head of an animal rights group. You'd think that a group that thought a rat, pig, dog and boy were equal could accept someone that was "differently vital." But no, they seemed to view it as just another version of human encroachment into the "pristine realm" of Gaia. The op-ed even claimed that he was disrupting the biosphere by not allowing his remains to "nurture the microbes of the Mother Earth."

The course director was a small man that spoke with great big gestures. With a flourish of hands and arms, he finished the introduction and Wissen stepped up to the lectern and cued his "wake-up" slide. "Stem Cells. Can't live with 'em, can't be Undead without 'em."

"Stem cells were much maligned in the early part of the century. There was much public outcry over the misconception that stem cells could only come from fetal tissue. People who opposed abortion were afraid that research in stem cells would fuel a need for more tissue, thus encouraging more abortions. Others were afraid of a rash of new cancers or birth defects." That usually got a few nods. It really hadn't been so many years since the government had lifted the total ban on stem cell research.

Wissen had been practicing the lecture with a voice recorder for the last week. Since the accident he'd tended to talk in a quiet monotone. It was an effort to add tone and inflection, but he thought he'd done a decent job. He quickly flipped through several slides showing how most cells in the human body can only form tissues composed of those same types of cells. This was the dull part—the basic background that needed to be covered before getting to the point of the lecture. "We've known for a long time that bone marrow makes a wide variety of very specialized cells; that whole human bodies form from just a few cell types in the fetus. These stem cells have the potential to replace damaged cells in parts of the body that just don't replace all that easily."

He looked around the lecture room. By this point in his career, not to mention the week of practice, lecturing was pretty well automatic. The mouth moved, words came out, but he really didn't have to pay much attention to what he was saying. Instead. he looked again at the distribution of students in the room. As expected, the students in the front rows were attentive. The ones in the back looked bored, but a few heads were up and listening. As he went on to describe the many sources of stem cells used in current research: bone marrow, amniotic fluid, umbilical cord blood, transformed endothelial cells, and only very rarely, fetal tissue, he noticed that many of the front row students were writing notes, but the back row students seemed to be distracted or were starting to talk among themselves.

"But what use are we to make of stem cells?  Our best example is the brain.  For years, scientists felt that a human brain was born with all of the neurons it would ever have—that no neurons could be added or regrown.  Now we know that certain areas of the brain, such as the dentate gyrus of hippocampus, have the ability to make new brain cells.  Most brain areas do not.  What if we could replace the neurons damaged by stroke, injury or disease? Like the old-time alchemists trying to turn lead into gold, the Neural Alchemist turns stems cells into any brain cells we need."

There was a stir in the back.  Usually by this point in any lecture there would be questions.  Medical students liked to gain recognition among their peers by asking questions that they hoped a lecturer couldn't answer.  The bragging rights of an unanswered question were a major contributor to student hierarchy. The two people who stood up in the back of the lecture hall didn't look like students about to ask a question, though.  For one, the standing male and female did not really look like students; most med students start off with a passing familiarity with personal hygiene and got better once they started performing patient exams.  These two looked downright scruffy, unbathed, and wearing dirty clothes.  What was that bag at their feet?

"NO ZOMBIES!" The female shouted.  The male reached into the bag and threw an elongated object.

It was an arm.  A severed human arm.  Every face in the hall turned toward the couple.

"UNDEAD.  EVIL.  NO BRAIN-EATING ZOMBIES!"

The barrage of limbs continued.  The man throwing them would certainly not make the big leagues.  Most of the limbs were falling in the vacant middle range of seats.  A foot made it far enough to hit one seated student in the head. His expression quickly cycled through horror, to revulsion, then pain.

*Ah,* thought Wissen. *Mannequin parts dressed and painted to look cadaverous.* A few of the students were getting up and approaching the couple, who now turned to exit the room.  The movement rapidly turned into a chase, quickly emptying the back rows and part of the front.

"I guess that means today's lecture is done," Wissen told the few remaining students.  "Read the assigned chapters and we'll reschedule for next week."

The disruption did have one positive outcome, the next morning there was a petition posted on the student bulletin boards all over campus:

"Got BRAINZ???" It read. "Support Professor Wissen. Support Science. Fight Ignorance." There was an accompanying petition. The Dean's office eventually reported over 1200 signatures.  Considering that the Medical and Graduate Schools had 500 students and around 1500 faculty and staff, it was a strong show of support. Wissen, however, spent most of the intervening week in a depressed mood, retreating once again to his old basement lab.  Only at the rescheduled lecture had full attendance, no disruptions, and a much higher percentage of eager, interested faces, did his black mood start to lift.

The lab was cold and dimly lit.  Strange that it should be cold in the summer and warm in the winter, but the central heating and cooling conduits had access doors for maintenance on this floor, and they didn't always seal well.  The lab had no windows, stained ceiling tiles, broken flooring, leaky water pipes, and uneven pressure in the air, gas and vacuum lines.  It was the least popular lab in the building, and was frequently called The Dungeon by the graduate research students.  In the months between his "death" and even after his reinstatement in the faculty, it had been "Emeritus Professor" Wissen's home and workplace in the basement of the old Pathology research building.  Someday it would be renovated, but since an endowment had allowed the University to build a new research laboratory building last year, the renovation had become a low priority.

John Wissen liked The Dungeon.  Restoration of his position and funding had been accompanied by assignment of decent research space in the upper floors of the same building, but the disruption at the lecture had convinced him to keep at least *some* research down here and not all in the new lab.  Besides, students didn't like the constant breezes from the HVAC and the smell of the vivarium on the same floor.  The privacy had allowed him to perform a few procedures out of view of the students.

Research is based on repeating experiments, but how to repeat the singular experience of Undead Professor Johannes A. Wissen, Ph.D.?  There was only one source of reanimated tissue, Wissen himself.  Obtaining a tissue sample for testing meant taking a piece of his own flesh; and while John was not averse to taking small samples, the process left wounds that did not heal.  Healing would have required him to be alive.

He retreated to the office in the back of the Dungeon.  At one time it had been used for light-sensitive experiments; thus, once the door closed, there was no possibility of being seen from the outer lab.  A large mirror was mounted on the back of the door. John lifted his shirt and stared for a moment at the reflection.  His reanimation after the automobile accident had been delayed long enough that the coroner had performed an autopsy.  His verdict: Cause of death was cardiac arrest due to rapid impact with a steering wheel.  Large incisions started near each shoulder, joined at the center of the chest, then extended down to the upper abdomen, forming a "Y."  It was stitched closed with precise black sutures, but the edges of the wound remained raw and reddened. Several smaller incisions were not as neatly stitched, marking the sites of previous samples that Wissen had performed himself.

The skin should be cold, gray and necrotic. *If I were truly a zombie, I'd look dead,* he thought. *Not warm and pink. Not red around the stitches.* There was no sign of bleeding at the incisions, the heart didn't beat, the blood didn't flow, but aside from unhealed scars, he looked as alive as he had ever been.

Today's sample was from the liver. He could get at that though the existing autopsy incision. He unwrapped the sterile covering of his surgical kit. *I don't know why I bother autoclaving it. It's not like I'm going to get an infection.* Using fine scissors, he snipped two sutures from the Y-shaped incision and inserted the biopsy probe. A quick twist captured the liver sample and he removed the probe and placed the tissue sample in a sterile culture dish.

A small drop of dark red blood lingered at the probe site. As he brushed it away to begin re-suturing the skin he realized how complacent he had become about the whole procedure. *Damn, I just stuck a whopping big needle into my abdomen without a second thought. I suppose that the lack of feeling—pain or emotion—makes it easier.* Replacing the sutures took only a minute. Looking in the mirror John tightened the silk thread and snipped off the excess with the scissors. As he moved to place the needle in a container for re-sterilization it slipped out of the grasp of the metal forceps. Reflex born of years of protecting delicate lab instruments caused him to grab at the falling needle. While he succeeded in arresting the fall, the sharp point of the needle jabbed through his protective gloves and deep into the palm of his hand.

*Ouch.* Wissen thought. *It's just as well that I can't feel that.* John had realized quite early in his new existence that he had very little sensation of touch or pain in his body. That fact had led to the next routine that Wissen performed while he was still alone and in front of a mirror. He pulled over a magnifying mirror similar to the kind used for applying makeup. Using the magnifier and door mirror, he examined each incision, then each patch of unbroken skin for new wounds and injuries. If he didn't want to become a horror movie cliché, he needed to bandage and repair each injury before he risked losing body parts. The new puncture wound in his palm didn't require closing, but it wouldn't hurt to put some tape over it for a few days.

Inspection complete, John exited the office and returned to the outer lab. He would prepare a small sample for microscopy then send the remainder upstairs for the students to culture. Looking at the tissue sample in the sterile dish, he again noticed the drops of blood.

Dark red blood, He thought. And that's the problem. Live blood should have gotten redder when exposed to air; dead blood should be dark brown or black. There had to be oxygen though; somehow oxygen was getting to his brain, muscles and skin without being carried by blood and circulated by the heart.

John dabbed a smear of blood on a slide and looked at it under the highest magnification he could manage on the old light microscope. More sophisticated tools were available in the upstairs lab, but this would do for now. *Red cells, white cells. That's normal. Those filaments, though... It COULD be fibrinogen, except for the fact that they usually show up in clotted blood and as the basis for scabs and scars. None of THAT is happening, so why are they there?* He moved the slide to a new location and adjusted the focus. *Those small cells look very similar to the stem cells he'd been working with prior to the accident. Still, they didn't look quite right, more like immature blood cells.* He'd have a technician run some cellular labeling assays to check it out.

John was not even aware that he had been scratching lightly where he had taken today's sample. Nor did he notice when he started pressing his palm against the edge of the lab bench to relieve the dull ache of the puncture wound.

One-week later John again entered the privacy of the downstairs lab. The recent liver tissue and blood had indeed included stem cells, along with more of the filaments—not just in the blood, but in the liver sample as well. In order to start sustainable cultures, he'd need a larger tissue sample and considerably more blood.

He was facing away from the mirror as he removed his shirt. As he turned around and reached for the sampling probe he stopped...

...and stared.

The incision immediately over the prior sampling site was closed. About an inch of new scar tissue had formed in the middle of the autopsy incision.

*I guess I'll have to go in from a different site.* He began to snip away sutures below the new scar and prepared to insert the slightly larger sampling probe. *DAMN. That HURTS!* He retrieved the probe and sample, but had to sit down and rest before attempting to suture the incision. He might have to try some anesthetic before collecting the blood sample.

Out in the lab he found an anesthetic spray used to desensitize incision sites during animal surgeries. The suture sites burned from the slight punctures of the needle, but the spray relieved enough of the sensation that John could consider the next step.

With no heart beat or blood circulation, it would not be possible to just stick a needle in a vein and draw blood. He had planned to make a longitudinal incision in a large vein near the ankle, and rely on gravity and pressure on the calf to squeeze enough blood into a test tube for culture. A quick test of the scalpel on the skin of the ankle revealed no sensation down there—yet. Still, he was reluctant to cut on himself and repeat the experience of the biopsy probe. This would require some assistance.

Phil Wohlrab had been a friend and occasional co-worker since college. John had spent a few years working in various labs before going to graduate school;

Phil had joined the Army, become a medic, and then went to medical school after being discharged. John had just joined the faculty when Phil arrived as a first year Internal Medicine resident. They'd rekindled their friendship and become like brothers, even to the point of helping each other through the pain of losing spouses. Most recently, Wohlrab was working with the Aging Center to address problems of administering medications to the elderly populations. He had extensive experience with patients having collapsed veins, so John called him in to assist.

The basement lab seemed crowded with John, Phil and Laura Diaz in it. John was seated in a reclining chair while Phil inserted a cannula into one of the large veins in John's neck.

"This is no different than a central line, John. I'll insert the tubing far enough that it should be at the right ventricle, then draw blood."

"Urgh," was all John could manage. Phil had placed a high collar around his neck to keep it in the appropriate position for the procedure.

"I think that was 'Thank You,'" injected Laura helpfully.

"No," gasped John, "that was 'Hurry up.'"

Phil drew 10 cc's of blood and then quickly removed the tubing. The blood in the syringe was dark reddish-brown, but the drop that formed at the entry site on the neck was a brighter red.

"Definitely oxygenated blood, John," said Wohlrab. He transferred the blood into a tube containing chemicals to preserve the sample, and then placed the tube in a bucket of ice chips. "Do you want me to take any other samples while I'm at it?"

"No," said John, removing the collar and massaging the neck muscles. "Either this is it, or I'll have to submit to a full surgical procedure to get all of the samples we'd need. Since I have no desire to repeat that autopsy, this had better be it. Thanks, Phil, you're a good friend."

Laura spoke up. "Did you know you actually *smiled* when you said that, John?"

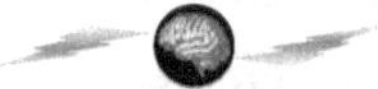

The International Union of Pathology and Pathophysiology was being held in Innsbruck, Austria. The Congress Centre was a bare half kilometer from the old city and former residence of Holy Roman Emperor Maximillian. The juxtaposition of old and new was never more apparent than in the modern teleconferencing facilities of the Salon where Professor Wissen was scheduled to address the conference. The legal issues had long since been resolved to the point where he could have travelled to the scientific meeting, but an excess of publicity coupled with recent developments made it safer to address his colleagues over a closed-circuit television link.

The university's teleconferencing studio was a strange mixture of television news studio and academic office. John sat at a desk in front of a video camera; in front of him, two video monitors showed the assembled scientists and the master of ceremonies beginning the introduction in Innsbruck. To one side of the desk was a computer which would control and display the presentation simultaneously in the local and remote locations. On the wall behind him were the University Medical Center logo, a white board, and a bookshelf with books arranged to prominently display key Pathology textbooks.

In Austria, the speaker was finishing the introduction: "...and without further delay, I present this year's Keynote Lecturer, Professor John Wissen." On that cue, John tapped the computer keyboard and started playing a video that had been prepared over the previous months in anticipation of this presentation. It started with him seated in this very studio, addressing the camera:

"Fellow Scientists. I won't dwell on the sensationalism and lurid background of this finding, but I am here to report that our research team has made an astounding discovery in stem cell research. For years we have known that life is an intricate balance of metabolism and movement. The mammalian system consists of a closed circulatory system that supplies individual cells with oxygen and glucose for their individual metabolic needs, and removes the organic wastes provided by those same metabolic processes. But what if we could remove the redundancy of identical chemical processes in each cell and simply supply the energy through a distributed network between cells? Individual cells would not metabolize, nor would they excrete, but they would all receive exactly the energy they needed in order to function.

"We have determined that specific differentiation of stem cell line UMC325 into a novel cell type that we call UMC325.JW provides just that function. JW cells consume oxygen and organic molecules and transfer the essential energy storing molecule—ATP—directly to any mammalian cells. JW cells are highly mobile and quickly permeate living tissues, leaving an interconnected matrix in their path. This matrix makes blood circulation, and even a beating heart, unnecessary. My unique existence is because of JW cells."

John watched the audience on the monitors as the video continue. There was much nodding of heads, whispered comments, and furious note-taking. The video continued with time-lapse recordings of the essential experiments that proved the thesis. Laboratory rats were injected with the JW cells, 24 hours later their hearts were stopped by electric shock. EEG and EKG monitors showed no activity, for 30 minutes. To all appearances, the lab rats were dead. Between 30 and 60 minutes after the heart shock, each laboratory rat began to twitch, move its limbs, and eventually get up and walk around. EEG tracings revealed renewed brain activity even though EKG showed a complete absence of heart beat.

The video proceeded to show repeated demonstrations with cats, dogs, and monkeys. *And that was when the real problems started,* John thought. Organizations that fought to prevent animal "death" in medical research were strangely unsympathetic to the fact that those same animals were brought back to "life" in Wissen's lab.  The protests and death threats had caused him to move out of his apartment and take up residence again in his basement lab.  At least the university had furnished it for him this time.

It's a good thing no one ever saw the final step in the progression.

Once it was determined that JW cells already present could return an animal from death, John knew that he would need to test whether they would be effective if administered to a creature—a human—that was already dead.  The problem was that legally, ethically, he could do nothing of the sort.  The Buckley incident was a rare accident, but it had nearly cost him everything.

Joseph Buckley was a computer tech for the university.  Three months ago, he'd had the unenviable task of babysitting the uninterruptible power supplies serving the computer room while University Engineering repaired the emergency power switch for that building.  Despite massive battery backups, each server was connected to the emergency power circuits to ensure that no data could be lost due to power interruptions.  During the switch repairs, Buckley had to make sure that the servers were running off of the batteries, or carefully shut them down with their data intact.  The power surge was unintentional, but it caused one UPS to fail catastrophically.  Fortunately for the computers in the room, the resultant arc found a closer path to ground; unfortunately for Buckley, his body completed that circuit.

John was enroute from the basement to his upstairs laboratory when the lights flickered and died.  He heard the scream from the computer room and was the first to arrive at the scene.  When he discovered that Buckley had no pulse, he realized he had to do something.  While he could not administer "mouth-to-mouth" resuscitation—after all, he had no "breath" to share—he could at least provide heart compression until the paramedics arrived.  After nearly an hour with no success, the paramedics declared Buckley dead and sent his body to the morgue. When Joe woke up screaming in a morgue drawer six hours later, all Hell figuratively and literally broke loose.

Without injection, without ingestion, and without any overt intent to use Buckley to test John's theories, somehow the JW cells had been transferred. The Ethical, Legal and Scientific Investigation Board determined that the transfer had occurred during the prolonged skin-to-skin contact during the CPR attempt. John had opened Buckley's shirt and placed his hands directly on his chest, providing a pathway for JW cells to migrate from Wissen to Buckley. Since that event, John had been in effective isolation and anyone in contact with him during the past months were subject to intense examination and distrust.

The video presentation was drawing to a close. On the computer screen, John's recorded image was talking about the unique metabolic requirements of JW cells. A red light flashed 5 times in the studio, and the "live video" indicator was displayed on all video screens.

"That video was prepared over the previous three months. You can now see why I was unable to attend the meeting in person." The audience members were visibly startled by the biological isolation suit, not to mention John's gaunt and withered appearance compared to the recording they had just viewed.

Wissen coughed, and resumed in a hoarse voice. "We have since learned that JW cells infiltrate brain, nervous system and muscle within hours. However, they do not appear in endothelium or the lining of the gut for many months. Until the digestive system is reactivated, the subject is unable to process or absorb nutrients from food. JW cells have a very efficient metabolism, but eventually the need for nutrients causes them to break down the very cells they have reanimated.

"For those who are encouraged by these breakthroughs, I must caution you that they are short-lived. For the many who are outraged and offended at my very existence, I can likewise assure you that it will soon end.

"I caution you, though.  I may have been first, but I suspect that I will be far from the last of my kind.  Knowledge, once found, cannot be undiscovered."

The video camera turned off, and the computer screen displayed a message that Professor Wissen would be unable to answer questions.  Further inquiries should be directed to office of sponsored research at his university.

Laura Diaz had been sitting out of camera view.  She quickly rose and came to Wissen's side to move his wheelchair as soon as the video feed was turned off.  "John.  You're weak.  Please eat; we both know what you need."

Wissen looked at his oldest, dearest, and possibly last remaining friend with sadness.  "No Laura.  There are some things that even a renegade scientist can't do, zombie or not."

"Yes, you can John.  This is a medical center.  There are ways.  It does _not_ have to be like this.  It's the _one_ thing we learned from Buckley."

"Oh, yes.  That will go over well.  The Vegan Revolution won't even let the native Scots eat haggis.  No, I've had my chance.  I can't do this anymore."  He refused to look at the tears in Diaz' eyes, but he took her hand and she said nothing.

The JW cells found in Buckley were much more developed than the unpurified cells which had originally accidently infected Wissen.  Buckley woke up in six hours compared to John's seventy-two.  Joe's second life lasted just two months to John's twenty-eight.

Of course, Buckley started having food cravings only 4 weeks after his reanimation.  The scientists would never know just how long he might have existed if he'd had continued access to food.

*I'll be damned if I let that happen to me.* Buckley had been literally dismembered by an angry mob after he'd been discovered bent over the bloody body, eating the heart of his latest victim. *Then again, I'm probably damned anyway. After all, I've lived more than two years in Purgatory, if not outright Hell.*

"Laura, promise me that you'll figure it out. Either figure it out, or destroy the JW cell line once and for all."

"Yes, John, I promise."

"Good. I would really rather not be remembered for unleashing zombies on the world."

Laura looked shocked. "Surely you don't think..."

Wissen sighed, and it sounded like a death rattle. "I do, Laura. 'Not with a bang,' nor a whimper, but a starving bloody madness. I just hope we're not too late."

But they were.

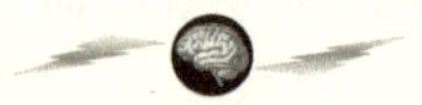

# THE WAR AND THE ROSES

*Authors note:  This was a different type of challenge story, and we meet up with a considerably older Skip Davis (from Operation Nightfall: Book 1 of the Campfire Tales), which also happens to occur in the future of my first stand-alone novel The Human Side (more to come on that story, too!). The story was going to be for a charity volume, and I decided to use it to push on a storyline I tentatively named The Prodigies.*

*Yeah, I have a lot of story lines being juggled here—not to mention at least three universes or variations thereof.*

*Still, this is another school story, this time at an exclusive prep academy for ex-tremely—talented—kids, and their rather mundane headmaster.*

*But not everything is as it seems.*

"What do you mean you can 'surf' a lake of liquid methane?"

"Well, you're gonna have to be in a pressure suit, right? ...and those things leak heat.  So, I designed my board to conduct heat to this point just forward of the ram jets. The methane vaporizes and floats the board. Now methane liquifies at 112 Kelvin and oxygen at 90 K, so there'll be a layer of LOX underneath. The scoops right here will mix a bit of LOX with methane vapor and push it into the combustion chamber. Burn methane and oh-two and you get thrust. All it takes is a bit of a push-off to start the flow, and you can do that with a foot or paddle."

The General stood bemused, listening to the youth demonstrate a surfboard for a planetary surface neither he nor the youth were ever likely to encounter. "Ah, yes, I'm sure that's very nice, young man. Thank you, but I suspect Mister Davis needs to show me..."

"Yes, indeed, General. Thanks, Ben, see you at dinner." Director Davis gritted his teeth at the general's condescending tone, but turned and led the visitor out of the machine shop and into the corridor.

As the door closed, the general stopped and turned to Davis, the bemused look and genial manner were gone. "Why do you let him waste his time on such nonsense? Surfing on Titan. Impractical and impossible. Pah, surely your government doesn't fund such nonsense."

Davis looked up into the taller man's eyes. "Impossible? Maybe, but that is the nature of the Institute. Impractical? Did you look at those thrusters General Brandt? Did you listen? He's talking about a ramjet that can be started with no more motion than a good push-off. The nozzle design is pure genius, and it doesn't require a lake of liquid methane. Look at it this way, spread the board shape into a delta, add a small fuel tank and you have a self-starting ramjet that can be dropped from a plane or launched from a catapult. The design works, the Dreamland folks have a prototype in final testing already. THAT is why the Institute allows our students to indulge in 'such nonsense.'"

Davis was breathing rapidly, and just a bit red in the face. The General looked him in the eye, then quickly looked away in embarrassment. ."..and General? It's Colonel Davis if you please, Doctor if you must. The Air Force was just as responsible for my being here as the Board of Directors. The kids may just be kids, but the chain of command still exists."

"Does it, Colonel? Do you even understand the concept? You run this Institute like a daycare or a madhouse. Coddling children and letting them do whatever they want. People have DIED in this war, Davis."

"DO NOT tell me about people dying in this war, General. I KNOW it! My son was due to rotate home from Moonbase when it was hit by that Alien beam. I was at Mars Colony when the first alien ship appeared. I lost a leg, a lung and my wife getting home! So DON'T presume to lecture me about the war!"

The general raised an eyebrow, but the remainder of the outburst didn't seem to affect his overall mood. "Hmph. Well, enough of this, then. I rather think we should go find that aide of mine... Colonel."

"Yes, General. His tour should be done by now, too. We should be able to find him in the cafeteria. This way, please..."

Davis and Brandt left the classroom wing by way of the greenhouse. Ordinarily the rich smells of fertile soil and growing plants was soothing to headmaster, but the disruption caused by the visiting officer had him rattled. The shortcut through the greenhouse allowed them to circumvent the entrance to the dormitory wing. There was no sense in exposing THAT situation just now. He looked around, satisfied that there was nothing obvious in the greenhouse that the general could criticize.

He was wrong.

"Your fish tank has gone bad," said Brandt, gesturing to a green-filled tank off to one side.

"Actually, that's algae, General" said a young girl in a wheelchair. She appeared to be about twelve, and was dressed in bright colors with a smock that held various tools for working in the greenhouse.

"Pond scum," sneered the general. He looked around at the various plants. ."..and pansies. I suppose you can at least grow your own food in this place?"

"Ah, no, sir. Not exactly. This is largely a recreational space. It's soothing to the students." Davis turned to the girl, "Molly, show the General what you've been working on."

Molly used her closed garden sheers as a pointer as she started naming the different varieties of orchids and roses around her. The Latin names sounded strange coming from a twelve-year old, but she pronounced them perfectly. ."..and my gardenias!" she finished proudly.

"I suppose it's too much to ask if you've weaponized the roses?" The general had been civil with the students so far, but now he made no pretense of hiding his irritation.

"No sir! They are pretty and they smell nice! I like sweet smelling flowers like some roses and my gardenias. I grow them because they make me feel happy." Despite her earlier facility with the scientific terms, Molly now pouted in the way that only a 12-year-old girl can master.

Brandt turned on Davis once again. "HAPPY doesn't win WARS, Colonel! HAPPY doesn't cure disease. HAPPY doesn't pay for this... this... 'toy factory'! MORE waste. Wouldn't your time and that of your so-called genius children be better spent trying to figure out how to FIGHT this war?"

Davis fumed. *He sees it, but doesn't understand it. Play is work to these kids... and work is play.* He gave an embarrassed smile to Molly, then nodded and steered the General toward the exit. Glancing back, he could see her maneuvering and raising the powered wheelchair and so that she could reach the back of the gardenia bush. *I suppose there's no sense explaining about the new medicines that Molly is working on, but I have to make him understand how wrong he is.* "They are CHILDREN, General, not robots. No matter how smart they are, they are not machines that can make whatever you want, whenever you want it!"

"You told me yourself that they aren't children, Colonel, they're geniuses. Geniuses that are consuming a lot of my budget, or it will be my budget in a few weeks. When that happens, you'd better stop growing pansies and pond scum and start making things we can use. We need weapons, we need defense against toxins, we need better field medicines, and you are just letting these expensive 'geniuses' play."

Davis responded in a tight voice, "You don't see it, do you? Did you notice the oxygen bottle on Molly's wheelchair? She has trouble breathing, but not in the greenhouse. She's deathly allergic to flowers, but she likes the ones that smell sweet. She thinks they're pretty, so that twelve-year-old bioengineered the antigens out of them! That 'pond scum' as you called it is Molly's version of Chlorella-B, the densest, most nutritious source of plant protein that exists. There's enough protein, sugars and essential fats in that small aquarium to feed even your fat ass for the next 10 years! And that 'child' grew all of it! She can feed your troops on a swimming pool full of bio'ed algae and you won't let her grow a few flowers?" *Got to keep it under control, calm down, take a deep breath, hold it, let it out.*

After a moment to calm himself, he continued. "Our funding and oversight agencies are quite satisfied, General. It won't be coming out of your budget, so you don't have to worry that we're taking up space and funds that you need. Your country and mine have agreed to pool our resources to fight the aliens, but that doesn't mean we have to do it the same way."

Brandt stiffened at the tone in Davis' voice. He stopped walking and turned to stare directly at the director with narrowed his eyes. "That's all very well, coming from you, Director, but High Command sent me here to evaluate and make recommendations. My recommendation is that the headmaster has no sense of chain of command; these 'geniuses' are nothing but spoiled children; and that coalition funds would be better off used for weapons design and fabrication than paying for children's toys." He turned his back on Davis and walked swiftly to the exit.

Davis contemplated grabbing the General by the arm and stopping him, but instead quickened his own pace and replied tightly, "This tour was a courtesy, Herr General. Nothing more. We don't answer to High Command, and as far as who we do answer to? Well, High Command answers to them."

The greenhouse opened onto the Commons, with the cafeteria positioned off to one side. Brandt's aide, Major Huerta, was surrounded by several teenaged female students. There were giggles from several of the girls as he took the gelatin cube one of them offered. He popped it in his mouth and smiled. "I see what you mean. It does taste like steak."

"Here, try this one..." one of the girls offered, holding out her hand. Davis ignored the giggling girls, but cast a glare at the slightly older woman behind them. *I'll speak to you later*, he mouthed. She made sure that neither the general nor major could see her, then stuck her tongue out at him. Davis tried very hard to keep a straight face.

"Major. We have no time for this." The General glared at the younger man, who tried to simultaneously snap to attention and swallow. The result was a coughing fit that did nothing to mollify the impatient general.

When the aide finally regained his composure, he opened his mouth to apologize, but the general was already heading for the door. Without looking back, he spoke as if to the air in front of him, "I'll be sending my report to High Command tonight, MISTER Davis. I'm sure your Agency will have their own copy of it soon after." ...and with that he was out the door, his aide struggling to keep up.

Davis turned to the girls. "Better head back to the dorm girls, and get rid of that 'body' before dinner, please?" The girls giggled, and headed back toward the dormitory wing to clean up for dinner and—hopefully—dispose of their anatomy lesson. The plate of gelatin cubes was left on a side table. Picking up the plate, Davis raised an eyebrow at his assistant. "Gelatin, Jenny? I know what you were doing." He popped one of the cubes in his mouth. Tasteless, just as he thought.

"He was a fool, Dee, just like his boss. Empty of head and empty of stomach. We satisfied both." Assistant Director Jennifer Barnes looked back defiantly. Her eyes blazed and the force of her anger seemed like a wall of heat.

"You were in his head... in his MIND, Jenny. You made him taste things that weren't there, did you REALLY think that through? He's compromised! If High Command were aware of it, he'd be stuck in a deep hole for the rest of his career. We're just lucky they can't stick us there with him."

"Nothing there, remember? He doesn't know anything, and he won't remember anything either. And I wasn't in his head. I didn't need to be, I got it all directly from him and his body language; he imagined everything on his own without any outside help. All he knows is that after a tour of the classrooms and grounds, a bunch of pretty teen girls from the Biofoods class asked him to sample a new type of ration cube."

"Dangerous, Jenny. If the general had noticed..."

"He didn't, Dee. I checked. He was so wrapped up in his own disgust that he wouldn't have noticed if all of the girls had flashed their cleavage at him. You worry too much; we have this handled."

Davis sighed. "I know you think I'm hopeless. You—all of you—are so far beyond everyone around you, that you think the rest of us 'Ordinaries' might as well be stuck in caves painting on the walls with charcoal."

"Well, aren't you? You're sweet, Dee, and the kids all love you, but even YOU aren't one of us."

"We've had this argument before, Jenny. This job is not just patronage for being a war hero. The Agency put me here. High Command wants me here. The Board even brought me out of retirement solely to direct the Institute."

There was a growing noise outside the Commons. It was nearly dinner, but the students seemed to be waiting for the argument to end. *Of course, they could hear it*, Davis thought, *and Jenny was probably projecting. Still, it's considerate of them to wait. Ah well, let them come in and give them the news.* As soon as he formed the thought, students started entering from greenhouse and dormitory. Jenny glared at Davis. The words "*This isn't over*" were as clear as if she had spoken them aloud. "It never is." Davis sighed.

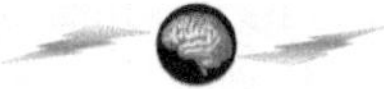

A few of the older students went to the cafeteria windows and collected large platters and bowls of food and returned to the tables. The kitchen staff prepared and served food throughout the day, but left before dinner. The Institute at dinner was not for the uninitiated.

A wide range of human mental potential came out on display, and it wasn't just the technical discussions. Fruit levitated itself from bowls and crisscrossed the room. A nine-year-old boy reached for a rare piece of meat, dripping with red—by the time it reached his plate it was fully cooked and sizzling. Here and there students conversed, laughed, argued; but in many other places, the kids were silent, making eye contact, nodding and occasionally making noises, but otherwise communicating silently. An older boy picked up rolls and began to juggle. As each object arced overhead, it alternately appeared and disappeared, describing intricate patterns which could only have been possible if the rolls were able to physically pass through each other.

Davis looked on proudly, yet could not help but feel a touch of sadness, knowing that the announcement he was about to make would mean an end to the happy chaos of the Institute. He waited through most of dinner, studiously avoiding Jenny's gaze. She had to know what he was about to say. In fact, it was likely the whole Institute knew, no matter how hard he worked to keep it out of his thoughts.

He stood up and the room fell silent immediately. Seventy-five solemn faces looked back at him. Well, no need for preamble. They know. "Uh-hum. Well... we knew this was coming, and now it has. The Agency and Board of Directors are going to put us to work. The General's visit today was no coincidence, it was intended that he would be deploying several of you with the orbital defense stations. That won't be happening, at least not for the reasons he thinks. Still, we are going to be split up, Skywatch thinks they've spotted alien activity in the outer system. Assistant Director Barnes will be taking her class to Farside to supplement the scanning crew. Brent," he nodded to the juggler, "will select five seniors to accompany him to the U.S.S. Carter in case we do make contact. The engineering and design class—that's you, Ben—will be going to Dreamland, but at least you will be able to come home with an escort team on weekends. Molly, I received a special request from Medical for your services, they wanted you to go back east, but I explained that your special care needs would be better met here. There will be a liaison arriving next week, don't let them talk you into relocating unless it's the lab on Kauai, you might even find that you like the smell of their hibiscus as much as your gardenias!" He winked in her direction. "The rest of you, well... the older students will be receiving assignments. Younger students will remain at the Institute under reduced staffing, but there will be at least two liaison teams on site. Be nice to the Ordinaries. They want your help, but they aren't really going to understand all of this."

Davis paused. The cafeteria was not quite silent, but there was a strange sensation. Not a physical or audible buzzing, nevertheless it was like straining to hear a distant conversation when you can't make out the words. *Ah. At least they're talking about it among themselves.* "You're going to have a lot to do to prepare, and a lot to say to each other. I figure you'll want a big party this weekend. Go ahead. You deserve it."

Instead of sitting back down, Davis turned and headed for the outside door. It would be best for the kids to leave them with just their own company for the evening. Jenny caught up with him just outside the door and touched his arm. He turned and saw a softer expression than before. "I don't need your pity, Assistant Director."

"Dee. You didn't mention what you will be doing," she said softly.

"As if you didn't already know? You can't see it?" He knew the bitterness was unfair, but after the argument earlier, he felt like pushing back.

"You know that of all people, I've never been able to read you."

"That's a blessing, Jenny, you don't EVER want to see what's inside this old dinosaur's head."

"Dee, I didn't mean what I said earlier..."

"No, you were right. I'm not one of you, Jenny, even if I helped mold you into what you are. You want to know what High Command said? They said they didn't need a broken down 'child minder' in Defense."

"But you said it yourself, Dee. High Command is not Agency, and we're not in their chain of command. So, you stay here, you still do valuable work. The Institute needs you; the kids need you. "

"No, I don't get to stay, either. The Board has not told me what I will be doing, yet. I just know it isn't here."

Jenny was silent for a moment. The racing thoughts were a little too obvious... She was going to Farside, he was going to some nebulous *elsewhere*... "Ok, so just who is supposed to be the new Director?"

It was enough to break the tense mood. Davis turned and glanced sideways at her, the ghost of a smile forming on his lips. "Well, Jen... It was supposed to be..."

"No! Not the General!"

"Nope, the Major. He was assigned as Brandt's aide last week once they scheduled the tour. The Board wanted him to look at us, and us to look at him, to see if he could handle it. Your little trick seems to suggest that's not such a good idea though."

Jenny looked horrified. "But... no... we didn't mean... I didn't mean..."

"It's okay, Jenny. He wasn't right for the job. Like the General, he just couldn't see the potential. I don't know, maybe they'll pull Mizz Stone out of retirement the way they did me." He turned to head across the grass to a small building that served as administrative office and quarters. "And now, I am tired. I'm sure I'll have a report due and plenty of correspondence with the Board before the day is over. Good night, Jen. Tell the kids to keep a lid on it. They can let off steam this weekend."

He felt her standing there a moment, then turn as he continued walking. *Good night, and good luck, Dee,* her thoughts came, softly.

Entering his office, Davis thought, Augh! I need a drink. I haven't felt I needed one since I took this job. After all, not a good idea to mix alcohol with the type of mental alertness needed with these kids. Still, a nice scotch would go well; pity there's been no one in Scotland to distill whisky since the last attack, the Japanese spirit is just not the same. It would just kill Dad to see the barren hills and empty cities where the alien death beams have touched. He settled for a glass of iced tea and sat down at his desk, preparing to write his report.

Noticing the red light flashing next to the large teleconference screen, he touched a control and a message panel informed him that the system was reconnecting with the last caller.  The screen lit up to show a familiar, yet worn and tired face.

"My God, Donnie, you look like hell!"

"You don't look so fresh yourself, Davis.  How's the leg?"

"Still hurts in cold weather.  How's the hand?"

The man in the screen held up his right hand.  Although encased in a black glove, it looked normal.  However, the slight whirring noise as he flexed and wiggled his fingers was not.  "You should know.  DARPA's best, and High Command still won't let me fly."  He grinned.  "Bastards!  Their loss.  So how were the visiting firemen?"

"A total wash.  Typical 'what have you done for us lately' mentality.  The General's too linear a thinker, he had no idea what he was seeing.  Patronized Ben, told Molly she was wasting time with her roses and gardenias.  The Major wasn't much better, the girls did their usual and he fell for it."

The caller sighed.  "Too bad, we had hopes for Huerta.  Very well, write it up and send it to the Board, then pack up and get out here as fast as you can."

"What, Dreamland?  I know I was sending a class out there..."

"You, too.  We need your whiz kids to do a bit of advanced design and reverse-engineering."

"I caught part of that, so what do you need me for?"

"We have a request for a doc with extreme environment experience, you've been specifically requested through Agency HR and they agreed.  That's the real reason your merry band is being activated.  We knew you'd never leave while you thought the kids weren't ready.  Besides, we were going to have to move all of them to a better facility soon."

"No barracks and guard houses, Donnie, you promised."

"Nope, state of the art campus, full telepresence facilities so that all the kids can contribute and we won't have to always break them up. We planned to do it next summer, but we're going to move it up as much as we can. Now get off the comm, write that report, and get your butt out here—and I do hope you're bringing Benjy. Kid reminds me of you when you were younger, Space Cadet."

"Yes, Sir, General. We'll be there next Monday. Got to throw the kids a party, after all."

"Agreed. Donald out."

Davis sat a moment at his computer, thoughts racing. A new project, something that required reverse-engineering, something that could take the battle to the aliens. The humans of Earth were going out to take back what had been stolen from them. About time, and he had just the kids to do it. Now, if only he didn't have this report to write... Damn, the leg hurts. He reached down, unstrapped the prosthetic and set it aside. Reaching for his iced tea, he realized it had gotten pretty warm. *Ah well, no one here to see.*

"Computer, dictation. Letter to Maryanne Stone, Chairman of the Board, Stone Institute for the Exceptionally Gifted. cc to Emerson Donald, Director, Homeworld Security Agency."

Across the room, the refrigerator door opened on its own, the iced tea pitcher floated across to the desk.

"Regarding the inspection tour and evaluation of General August Volker Brandt. Evaluation of Major Odalis Huerta will be delivered in a separate report. Evaluation of Brandt follows..."

Davis poured cold tea into his glass and mentally sent the pitcher back to the refrigerator.

"I am afraid that the good general failed his evaluation today..."

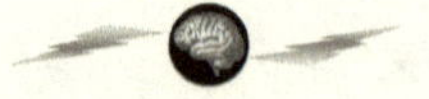

# Acknowledgements

Lower Education, Blood Science, and The War and the Roses were originally written as writing exercises, and used at various times as fill for my blog, or as free-sample "reader magnets." Neural Alchemist was the first time I sold a full-length story outside my circle of SF author friends. Hunter has languished in my To Be Finished pile since those early years, and I figured this was as good a time as any to finish it.

As I was putting together this collection, it occurred to me that these were all "Tedd Roberts" stories, and that they fit a trope I've personally had a bit of trouble overcoming—that of the college/university professor.

So why not take advantage of it?

The middle three stories—Blood Science, Hunter, and Neural Alchemist—were the result of challenge to break out of the mold of strict hard SF and try my hand at fantasy. Well, that only partially succeeded, but still, the stories make a nice collection of what we can call "Science-Fantasy."

On that note, many, many thanks to Sarah A. Hoyt, a friend and mentor who was the one to issue the challenge to write outside my ivory tower. Sarah taught me several important lessons—First, "take a chance, and just *write*." Second, when asked to contribute a story, never say "I don't write that." Instead, say "How many words? How much does it pay? When do you need it?" The third, more subtle lesson was to never be afraid to make fun of myself, thus, you will see that many of these protagonists could easily be Mary Sue/Marty Stu—if I wasn't having too much fun satirizing the trope.

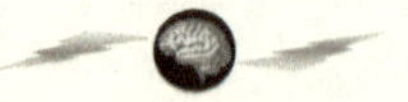

# About the Author

Doctor Robert E. Hampson is a Neuroscientist and author. By day, he is a professor at Wake Forest School of Medicine, studying how our brains encode memory. By night, he writes military, adventure and hard-science Science Fiction as well as nonfiction articles explaining science to the general public.

Robert Hampson's SF writing career began with "They Also Serve," a short story in Riding the Red Horse, published in 2015. That story became the foundation of his first solo novel The Human Side, in 2020. He has three collaborative novels with Sandra Medlock, Chris Kennedy and Casey Moores in the "Wrogul's Oath" arc of the popular Four Horsemen Universe. A final book in this arc is expected in late 2023.

Rob's latest novel is *The Moon and the Desert,* an updated retelling of The Six Million Dollar Man. In addition to novels, he has co-edited two anthologies, and published more than 25 works of short fiction (some written as "Tedd Roberts"). He is also a regular contributor of nonfiction articles for science fiction readers, with more than 15 articles published. One of the articles, "Why Science is Never Settled," was nominated for the Hugo Award in 2015 as Best Related Work. Hampson has sequels in the works to both solo novels, the Wrogul's Oath, and The Founder Effect anthology.

Doctor Hampson's forty-year scientific career has ranged from studying the effects of commonly abused drugs on memory, to the effects of space radiation on the brain. His current work, as lead scientist for Braingrade, Inc., is developing a medical device to restore human memory function damaged by injury or disease.  He is also a professor of physiology/pharmacology and neurology at Wake Forest School of Medicine where he teaches regularly in the neuroscience and biomedical graduate curriculum.  He also developed and teaches a course on Communicating Science, in which young scientists practice writing for—and speaking to—the general public.  He is a scientific journal editor; a reviewer for dozens of journals and research agencies; has been interviewed on his research by newspapers, radio and TV; a consultant to TV and game producers, defense contractors, and authors.  He has published more than 175 peer-reviewed scientific articles.

Hampson graduated in 1988 with a PhD from the Bowman Gray School of Medicine of Wake Forest University in Winston-Salem, NC.  He has worked as a newspaper carrier, greeting card merchandizer, computer data entry operator and programmer, and laboratory technician, and lived in Pennsylvania, Texas, and North Carolina.  He now lives in the Piedmont of North Carolina with his wife, Ruann.

Robert E. Hampson is available as a consultant through SIGMA—the Science Fiction Think Tank and the Science and Entertainment Exchange (a service of the National Academy of Sciences). His website is .

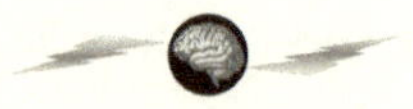

# Books by Robert E. Hampson

**The Moon and the Desert**

**Baen Books**

ISBN 978-1-982192-49-5

What would it really take to make the Six Million Dollar Man? a medical thriller on earth and in space!

Glenn Armstrong Shepard had his sights set on going to Mars as a flight surgeon, but a training accident on the Moon left him crippled. Now he has a new plan: to be fitted with bionic prosthetics and come back even stronger.

Fate and the Space Force have other plans, and Glenn is grounded. Another doctor—his ex-fiancée—takes his place, and Glenn will have to fight to prove he can be an astronaut once more. . .

## The Human Side

## Theogony Books

ISBN 978-1-648550-70-6

Is it an asteroid...or a weapon?

An asteroid headed toward Earth was not unexpected; multiple asteroids were a different story. And, when the "rock-throwing aliens" finally appeared, the people of Earth had to deal with a new type of war, where an enemy with powerful weapons held the high ground of space.

Doctor Tobias Greene felt guilty over patching up soldiers only to have them return to battle—until learning that his work was essential to the survival of the human race.

Master Sergeant Martin was a combat medic, trying to do his job and save as many as he could.

Lab Technician Kat Smith was forced out of her home and away from friends and family by the alien attacks. Her work was important, but would it be enough?

Jan and Li Janacek were trapped in New Mexico with their son, daughter, and eight other teens. They needed to get home...but home was no longer there.

For Arielle French, the aliens' arrival was everything she had predicted, until they attacked. Had she misunderstood their motives, or was it all the fault of the humans who failed to behave the way the aliens expected?

Technical breakthroughs might allow humans to resist the worst the "Rockers" could throw at them. But even if they could level the battlefield, though, would there be enough time left for Earth to show the Rockers what was really on the Human Side?

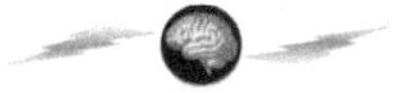

# The Founder Effect (Anthology, edited with Sandra L. Medlock)

## Baen Books

ISBN 978-1-982125-09-7

AWARD-WINNING AND BEST-SELLING AUTHORS CONTRIBUTE NEW STORIES: All-new fiction from Dragon Award winner and New York Times best-selling author David Weber, Dragon Award nominee D.J. Butler, best seller Jody Lynn Nye, indie best sellers Chris Kennedy and Mark Wandrey, and more. Also featuring an introduction by multi-award-winning and New York Times best-selling author Larry Correia.

It is 2185 CE. Humans now live throughout the Solar System, but their most ambitious adventure is about to begin. The starship Victoria will carry over 10,000 colonists to a new world outside the Solar System. The larger-than-life exploits of those colonists will become legendary. The colonists will build a new civilization, and the actions of a few individuals will become famous—and infamous—forever marking their new colony with the Founder Effect.

Contributors: Larry Correia, Mark H. Wandrey, Les Johnson, Christopher L. Smith, David Weber, Daniel M. Hoyt, Brad R. Torgersen, Monalisa Foster, Sarah A. Hoyt, Chris Kennedy, Vivienne Raper, Jody Lynn Nye, Brent M. Roeder, Catherine L. Smith, Philip Wohlrab, D.J. Butler

## Stellaris: People of the Stars (Anthology, edited with Les Johnson)

## Baen Books

ISBN 978-1-481484-25-1

NEW STORIES AND ESSAYS FROM TOP AUTHORS AND EXPERT SCIENTISTS. Explorations of how interstellar travel may affect humanity by best-selling authors and scientists.

The stars will change us.

STELLARIS: PEOPLE OF THE STARS is a collection of original science fiction stories and nonfiction essays speculating about humanity's far-term expansion into the universe beyond the limits of our solar system—with an emphasis on the changes humans will undergo as a species as we make this happen. Is interstellar travel so far beyond our current imaginings that it will take a fundamental transformation of humanity in order to make it possible? And, if so, will we remain Homo sapiens or become a new and unique species—Homo stellaris (the People of the Stars)?

Herein are original science fiction stories by award-winning authors such as Kevin J. Anderson, William Ledbetter, Todd McCaffrey and Sarah A. Hoyt, supplemented by accessible nonfiction essays describing the science behind the fiction from people who should know—Sir Martin Rees (Astronomer Royal of the United Kingdom), Mark Shelhamer (Chief Scientist for the NASA's Human Research Program), and more.

This collection of original stories and essays was inspired by a gathering of scientists, science fiction authors, and futurists at a series of annual meetings held by the Tennessee Valley Interstellar Workshop. Let their speculations, imaginations and boundless sense of what's possible take your own journey beyond the edge of the solar system in STELLARIS: PEOPLE OF THE STARS!

Stories and Provocative Speculation from: Sir Martin Rees, Kevin J. Anderson, Sarah A. Hoyt, Mike Massa, William Ledbetter, Todd McCaffrey, Kacey Ezell and Philip Wohlrab, Dan Hoyt, Les Johnson, Robert E. Hampson, Mark Shelhamer, Brent Roeder, Jim Beall, Cathe Smith.

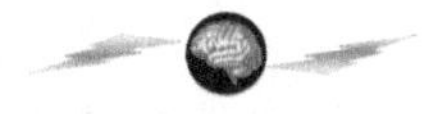

# The Wrogul's Oath

**Four Horsemen Universe Books by Robert E. Hampson and Sandra L. Medlock**

**Do No Harm (Robert E. Hampson and Chris Kennedy with Sandra L. Medlock)**

ISBN 978-1-950420-11-7

When Todd's critically damaged ship dropped out of hyperspace near the Human colony world of Azure, he had no memory of his past. He didn't know who he was, or even what he was, and the Humans didn't either. That didn't stop the colonists of Azure—they took him in, anyway...even though they didn't understand how he could do some of the things he could do.

Todd and his descendants consider themselves Human—eight armed and water-breathing—but Human, nonetheless. After seventy years living among Humans, Todd's descendants are going back out into the Union to make their mark—from fifteen-year-old Verne, who's a little short to be a mercenary, to Harryhausen, who wants to be the most famous PI in the galaxy. Eventually they learn that the rest of the Galactic Union knows them as Wrogul, intelligent octopus-like beings known for science and the ability to perform surgery like no other race can.

These Wrogul do more than just practice medicine, but they still intend to do no harm. Unfortunately, the Humans, whether they have two arms or eight, have powerful enemies... and the Wrogul may have no choice.

## And Break It Not (Robert E. Hampson and Sandra L. Medlock)

ISBN 978-1-648551-92-5

The planet of Azure is nearly idyllic—there is a high standard of living, industry is booming, and the two races—Human and Wrogul—get along well with each other most days.

But underneath it all, there is tension between the races. Despite having no reason for it, the Humans don't always trust the Wrogul, and there is a faction within the Wrogul community that doesn't want its young growing up "Human."

When a large group of Wrogul move into the ocean and strange things begin happening—weird lights seen in the depths and sabotage at the mariculture stations—the Human's distrust becomes outright suspicion of treachery.

As things spiral out of control, another force enters the system—a group ostensibly sent by the UN on Earth to inspect the crops being grown on Azure—which threatens to destroy everything the Humans and Wrogul have worked for.

While the Wrogul still intend to do no harm, the Humans have powerful enemies in the galaxy, and, this time, the Wrogul may have no choice about whether to join the front lines with their Human friends. Will the threat of a common enemy break the relationship between the Humans and Wrogul...or break it not?

## As My Witness (Sandra L. Medlock and Casey Moores with Robert E. Hampson)

ISBN 978-1-648554-17-9

Azure Colony avoided the larger conflicts of the Omega War and Guild Wars, only to fall prey to rogue mercenaries. Now they're rebuilding, but strange forces are at work. New friends on the ground and mysterious lights in the sky promise "interesting times" for the Humans and hyper-intelligent Wrogul of Azure.

Meanwhile, mercenary leader Verne and Peacemaker Harryhausen resume their search for the ancestral home of Azure's Wrogul. They encounter distrust, deceit, and misdirection from the all-powerful guilds, but they manage to learn of sightings of Wrogul-like aliens. Their strongest lead takes them to a forgotten system where a lost Human colony coexists with a strange alien race with remarkable similarities to the Wrogul.

But when they find the colony is in the middle of a civil war, they're forced to make a choice—do they choose sides or stand by while the colonists slaughter each other?

## This I Swear (Sandra L. Medlock with Casey Moores and Robert E. Hampson)

Forthcoming in 2023—the surprising conclusion to Todd's search for his ancestors.